MYSTERY

Fiction

Goulart, Ron, 1933-

Now he thinks he's dead
1992.

Now He Thinks He's Dead

Also by Ron Goulart

Even the Butler Was Poor
A Graveyard of My Own
The Wisemann Originals

Now He Thinks He's Dead

Ron Goulart

Walker and Company
New York

First published in the United States of America in 1992
by Walker Publishing Company, Inc.

Published simultaneously in Canada by Thomas Allen & Son
Canada, Limited, Markham, Ontario

Library of Congress Cataloging-in-Publication Data
Goulart, Ron.
Now he thinks he's dead / Ron Goulart.
p.   cm.
ISBN 0-8027-3220-8
I. Title.
PS3557.O85N68   1992
813'.54—dc20   92-7857
CIP

Printed in the United States of America
2 4 6 8 10 9 7 5 3 1

Now He Thinks He's Dead

$\triangledown$

1

H<small>E ONLY LIVED ABOUT</small> three minutes after he was hit. Just long enough for him to remind her that he'd been right.

It happened just short of one in the afternoon on a gray, overcast day in early June. The place he died was the parking lot of the Dahlman Publishing Building, overlooking the Saugatuck River in the town of Brimstone, Connecticut.

H. J. Mavity had arrived there a half hour earlier and parked her aging car near the curving strip of green grassy border that ran alongside the river. Gulls were circling ominously high up in the sooty sky, and out on the gray water a couple of pudgy Boy Scouts were paddling by in a canoe.

After unbuckling, H. J. stretched up to inspect herself in the cracked rearview mirror. She was a slim, pretty woman with auburn hair worn long. In just a little over a week, she'd reach the advanced age of thirty-two.

Groaning slightly as she contemplated her vanished youth, H. J. slid out of the car, walked around its dented front end to the opposite side, and tugged the door open. Then she grabbed her large black imitation leather portfolio off the passenger seat by its mended plastic handle and hefted it out into the gray afternoon.

"Here I am on the brink of middle age," she said to herself

as she went walking across the parking lot, noting that all of the thirty some cars sitting there were newer and in better shape than hers. "Here I am about to commence the slide down into the matron class, and what I've been lately is the artistic equivalent of a hooker." In the portfolio that was swinging in her left hand were three cover roughs for the new Dahl Books line of Regency romances.

The three-story glass and redwood building loomed in front of her. The low decorative hedges that circled the small red brick courtyard looked stunted and sick. Sitting in the wide space reserved for the publisher himself was old Oscar Dahlman's glittering black, blind-windowed limo. There was no way of telling if anyone was inside.

"Damn it, I studied art in Paris *and* Los Angeles," H. J. reminded herself as she went up the five red brick steps to the wide glass door that had "Dahlman Publications" etched on it in small sans serif lettering. "And if things work out I won't have to keep painting covers for tripe like *Love's Claimant*."

The reception room was large, oval, and extremely chilly. The pale blue walls were covered with tastefully framed covers of the various Dahlman magazines—*Cyclemania, Eat Right, Puzzlewit, Muscleman, Musclewoman, Bare, Bare Forum*. Near the pink marble fountain at the big room's center stood a six-foot-high plush replica of the lecherous grizzly bear, complete with top hat, who served as the mascot for *Bare*.

On her knees beside the dry fountain was a plump black woman wearing a bright orange dress. Standing near her was a plump, balding man in his middle forties. An attaché case dangled from his right hand.

"If it were a motorcycle," he was explaining to the kneeling woman, "I could fix it in a jiffy."

"They're going to blame me," she said. "I mean, I was only just trying to turn the water down some so the spray wouldn't spritz all over my desk. And it up and dies entirely."

"Try turning the same handle you used to turn it off. But in the opposite direction."

"Oh, now there's a bright suggestion. You must be a graduate with honors from the Plumbers' Academy. I've been turning the damn handle, but nothing whatsoever happens."

"Actually I went to Yale. Didn't become interested in motorcycles until I was past forty."

"Excuse me." H. J. approached the malfunctioning fountain. "Are you the new receptionist?"

"Not for long if I can't get this fountain working again."

"You have to kick it." H. J. booted the base of the fountain at the place where the handle was connected.

After a few seconds it started producing loud wanging noises. Then, after shivering and rumbling, the water came gushing up out of the mouth of the dolphin at the fountain's apex.

"Terrific." Getting to her feet, the receptionist brushed at her knees and then looked H. J. up and down. "If you want to pose naked for *Bare*, hon, what you have to do is leave your—"

"I'm flattered," cut in H. J., holding her large portfolio up higher, "but actually I make most of my living with my clothes on these days. I'm an artist and I have an appointment with Lloyd Dobkin."

"Oh, sorry if I offended you, hon. See, it's just that we get a lot of bimbos in here off the street looking to make some easy money as skin models." Smiling, she walked over and squeezed in behind her wing-shaped desk. "Who was that you said you wanted to see?"

"Lloyd Dobkin. He's editor-in-chief."

The balding man cleared his throat. "You are, if I may say so, attractive enough to be a model, miss."

"Why, thank you." H. J. glanced at him with her left eye narrowed. "I'll treasure that remark."

"Dobkin. Dobkin. Bingo, here he is." The receptionist was scanning a list. "Dobkin is extension twenty-six." She pushed buttons on her phone and waited.

"I myself write for *Cyclemania*," explained the man as he settled into one of the reception room chairs.

"I've been painting, somewhat against my will, for the new paperback division. Mostly romances."

"Hello, Mr. Dobkin? You're not? And this isn't extension twenty-six? Oh, thirty-six, sorry." She smiled at H. J. "I'll give him another try."

H. J. smiled back. "He's expecting me for lunch," she said. "I can just go on back to his office."

She looked from the phone to H. J. "Sure, you seem to be trustworthy and reliable," she said. "Go on."

"Nice meeting you," called the motorcycle writer.

H. J. pushed through the door that led to the first-floor office area.

She smelled Larry Dahlman before she saw him. Up ahead in the pale blue corridor an office door opened and a wave of the powerful aftershave that he apparently marinated himself in came fuming out.

H. J.'s nose wrinkled.

Larry was a large, rumpled man in his late thirties, blond, amiable, and built along the lines of the *Bare* grizzly. "Hi, Helen. You're looking great, as always." He stopped dead in her path, shifting the canvas bag he was carrying from his right hand to his left, held out the right.

Instead of shaking hands, she brushed at the air space between them. "I don't imagine you're bothered by mosquitos much," she observed. "Or probably any other flying predators up to and including condors."

He lowered his hand, grinning. "My aftershave is too strong, you think?"

"A wee bit."

"It's supposed to give me a bold and extremely masculine aroma."

"I'd ask for a refund as soon as possible."

Chuckling, Larry shifted his bag to his right hand again. "Well, I've got to go change."

"Still running on your lunch breaks?"

"Yeah, and I'm up to five miles a day now. I feel absolutely great, Helen." His grin grew wider. "I go out and run two and a half miles straight up Rivergate Road and then I run two and a half miles back."

"I guess you'd have to, otherwise you would never end up here."

"Probably nobody would miss me if I did fail to show up," he said. "Certainly not my sister and her dear husband. Dad doesn't rate me very high either." He lowered his voice. "He's lurking around the offices today."

"You shouldn't downplay yourself, Larry. You hold a responsible job in the family business."

"As an associate editor of *Bare* and *Bare Forum?*" He shook his head. "A couple of second-rate skin mags read exclusively by morons whose idea of a social life is to lock themselves in the john with a copy of the magazine." He shook his head again, more forlornly. "Say, I heard some unhappy news about you."

"Which?"

"Rumor that you were getting married again or something," he said. "Just when I was working up the nerve to ask you to dinner. I can't do that now, of course, because I don't fool around with married women."

"Actually I'm not exactly getting married. But, as fond as I am of you, you'd have to be perhaps not the last man alive on the face of the earth but at least among the final six or seven before I'd willingly plop myself down across a dinner table from you."

He laughed. "Well, no more kidding around. I've got to change into my running togs. Have a nice lunch with Lloyd." Patting her arm, he headed for the rest room.

She heard Eva Dahlman Dobkin before she saw her, the woman's voice, loud and harsh, sounding around a bend in the corridor.

"You're absolutely full of crap!" Eva was shouting, apparently in the open doorway of Dobkin's office. "Not just full of crap, Lloyd my dear, but overflowing."

"Okay, okay, love."

"Of all the insane things I ever did, and there were very

few before the dark day when you came slouching into my
life, marrying you was the dumbest, wackiest—"

"Think how I feel, pet. I'm only your second mistake, but
you're my fifth."

H. J. halted on her side of the bend, not wanting to walk
into another quarrel between her editor and his wife.

"I really just wish you'd cease to be," continued Eva.
"That you'd be stricken with some slow, painful blight. Or
that one of those disease-ridden floozies that you sleep
around with behind my back would either stab you, shoot,
you, or infect you with a dose of something fatal."

"We'll talk some more about the makeup of the October
Puzzlewit after lunch, Evie."

"God, I wish voodoo worked. I'd be sticking pins in your
effigy until—"

"Scoot back to the sanctity of your office and calm down.
I'll venture into your den later this afternoon."

"Screw you!" The door slammed, and Eva's angry foot-
steps filled the halls.

H. J. resumed walking.

She almost collided with Eva as she turned into the hall
that led to Dobkin's office. "Oops."

"Oh, hello, dear," said Mrs. Dobkin, smiling. She was a
large, wide woman, unbelievably blond, and a few years beyond fifty. "I don't know why you dress up so prettily to have
lunch with that toad."

"Now and then a toad turns out to be a prince."

"Ugh, you'd have to kiss him to make that happen." Eva
pressed the folder she was carrying tight against her bosom.
"May I give you some good advice, Helen Joanne?"

"Such as?"

"I've heard you intend to remarry that onetime husband
of yours. Ben Whoever."

"Ben Spanner. That's one of the options we're considering, yes."

"Don't do it. Wander out into the desert and live in a cave, get a part time job in a leper colony. Anything is better than marriage." She went striding off.

H. J. was still two paces from Dobkin's door when it opened a few inches. "She may just get her wish," he said by way of greeting as he opened the door wider.

H. J. crossed the threshold. "Her wish about what?"

"My leaving," he answered, "this world behind."

$\triangledown$

2

GRUNTING, DOBKIN SCOOPED A substantial bundle of photos of naked young women off the chair. "Sit for a while, H. J.," he invited.

"Don't you ever worry you'll suffer from an overdose of bare flesh?"

He was a lean, pale man of nearly sixty. What little hair he had left was concentrated in grayish tufts over his prominent ears. "These are the entries for the November 'My Best Girl' section of *Bare*."

"People actually do that, huh? Send in pictures of their wives and lady friends in the nude?"

Dobkin elevated the stack of pictures to chest level before depositing it atop his massively cluttered desk. Some 35-mm slides dropped free and fell to the thick tan carpet. "Haven't I assured you of that on several prior occasions?"

"You have, but I still find it difficult to believe. I guess I don't want to admit there are so many half-wits out there."

He squatted to gather up the slides. "This pile is only the cream, as it were, of the crop," he told her. "Larry winnows through the hundreds of 'My Best Girl' submissions and picks out a few dozen likely candidates. Then I select the ten girls we'll actually use per issue. I have to get them to sign release forms and so on." He held one of the rescued slides up to the overhead lights. "Now that's zoftig."

Resting her portfolio against the chair leg, H. J. crossed over to the nearest office wall to scan the framed photos and certificates. "Got cobwebs on your Edgar Award from the Mystery Writers of America." She brushed at the glass with her fingertips.

"Do you suspect there's some symbolism in that, my child? That it's maybe been too long since I was a top-seeded fact crime writer?" He leaned his buttocks against the edge of his desk. "Have you, speaking of past glories, read the copy of my book that I gave you?"

"Not exactly," she admitted. "But it's near the top of my must-read pile. I do like the title—*Great Kidnappings in America.*"

"*Great American Kidnappings,*" he corrected. "It was a substantial hit back in 1983, but then so was I. Is that stack of books reposing beside your bed at your cottage or over at Ben's?"

She sat, smiling at him. "I'm in the process of moving in with him full time. But I still sometimes use my old studio at the cottage for painting."

"Ben's okay," the editor observed. "I've always liked him."

"I'll tell him. It'll brighten his otherwise drab life and take his weary mind off the tons of money he's earning."

"You need a man with a skin as thick as Ben's. Not everybody can take living with a wiseass like you."

"I saw something to that effect in 'Dear Abby' only last week. What were you and Eva brawling about this time?"

"Same old stuff. We loathe each other." He made a sad sound. "Well, come on and show me your roughs for the *Love's Claimant* cover."

"You don't have to stay with Eva . . . or keep working here at Dahlman, do you?"

"No, no. Matter of fact, I've been offered a tin cup and a very warm corner in Manhattan," he said. "Actually, H. J., it's not that easy for an old codger like myself to go out and

earn the sort of money I pull down hereabouts. Which is why
I try to put up with Eva and her sweet-smelling younger
brother and her doddering old pappy. Old Oscar, by the way,
is making one of his fortunately rare visits today." He
straightened up, glanced at the door, and then the window.
"However, I may be on the brink of . . . let's simply say immense wealth."

"Not another of your schemes, Lloyd?"

Shaking his head, Dobkin tapped the stack of photos.
"The only thing I can tell you is that I owe it all to 'My Best
Girl.' "

"How exactly?"

"I can't discuss that with you just yet, even though I trust
you like a sister," he replied. "No, actually I trust you more
than that. My sister Inez was far from reliable. If she were,
she would never have held on to a name like Inez. Anyway,
my scheme, as you dub it, got going because of a lucky
chance." He touched at the corner of his right eye. "The fact
that I'm a perceptive old coot helped, too."

"I've recently had, as you know, some experience with a
get-rich-quick plan. Most of them turn out to be dangerous."

"This particular venture doesn't involve anything shady
or illegal—at least not on my part," he assured her as he
reached for the portfolio. "It does, I am at liberty to inform
you, make use of my considerable skills as a writer, investi-
gative reporter, and promoter. Soon, if all goes well, there will
be a best-selling true crime book of mine wowing the nation.
Followed by a docudrama on the tube and lord knows what
other lucrative spin-offs."

"All that because of a naked woman?"

Grinning, he flipped the big portfolio open and plucked
out the three cover roughs. "These are all lovely, H. J.," he
told her. "I see you took my advice about how to depict St.
Swithin's Church in the wilds of Sussex."

"Yeah, I used the Brimstone Denominational Church for
the model. Worked out pretty well."

"It looks great," he said. "You know, I love that old church.

It's so impressively grim and moldy. If I weren't a godless heathen, I'd drop in there some afternoon to rattle off a prayer, light a candle or, at the very least, rob the poor box. I might even haunt their old tumbledown graveyard." He held one of the roughs toward her. "We'll go with this one for the cover painting. Don't bother with a color comp, just go to the painting. Oh, and give me more cleavage on this innocent wench in the Empire gown."

"You sure you aren't getting the Gossamer Library of Regency romance mixed up with *Bare?*"

"Hey, everything sells better with extra cleavage." He consulted his watch. "Is Arnie's deli okay for lunch?"

"Sure, as long as you don't have two pieces of cheesecake this time."

"Promise." Dobkin made his way around the desk. From a lopsided, eagle-topped hatrack, he grabbed a tweedy sportcoat. "Also I'd like you to do me a favor."

"Okay, what?"

After shrugging into the coat, he opened the top drawer of his desk. He extracted a nine-by-twelve-inch manila envelope. Its flap was sealed with a wide swatch of brown tape. "Keep this for me in a safe place." He handed it across to her.

"Are you going to tell me what's in it?"

"Something I think is valuable. I want to have at least one spare, in case they find my files."

"Lloyd, it would be smarter, really, not to get yourself involved with something that—"

"I'm already involved. I can't get off now."

She dropped the envelope into her open portfolio. "Before we head for lunch, tell me what you meant about leaving this world. Have you been sick?"

"I know I told you about that attempt on my life last week."

She studied his pale face. "I thought maybe that was just one of your jokes."

"Somebody stretched a wire, low, across the top of the stairway." Dobkin touched his chest and then his ribs. "I plummeted down an entire flight of stairs and suffered, according to my overpriced Westport medic, an injury to the chest wall. It could've been a hell of a lot more serious if I'd fallen differently. And I'm near certain that's what they intended."

"Is this the same *they* who figure in all those paranoid delusions people have?"

Dobkin answered, "It all has to do with . . . well, with this research project I'm involved in. I started digging about a week and a half ago. But I don't think they got wind of it until a few days later, and that was probably my fault. They made their first attempt right after that."

"Couldn't it just have been Eva who stretched the wire?"

"This incident didn't occur at home. I thought I gave you all the choice details when you dropped in last week," he said. "It was at the palatial home of a lady who's young enough to be my daughter and whose husband is away on an extended business trip in Tobago. I was departing her bedroom when it happened."

"Still could've been Eva, if she knew where you were."

"She doesn't. Trust me."

"How about the young woman herself?"

"Micki's too dim to plan anything like that. Cute, but no Mensa candidate."

"Isn't Micki the one I saw you with at the Athena Diner that time?"

He lowered his voice. "No, no. You met Terri."

"I guess I made the mistake because she seemed dim, too," said H. J. "Did you, by the way, say that was only the *first* attempt? You never told me about a second."

"That took place over the weekend."

"At Micki's again?"

"No, this was . . . well, somewhere else. I left there about eleven. Her house, see, is up at the top of a steep, winding hill in Redding Ridge. On the way home my brakes went out."

"That could be because—"

"Nope, I had a complete tune-up just a month back. Somebody deliberately drained my brake fluid."

"But still . . ."

"If I hadn't managed to drive off the road, into a ditch and then across a bumpy field to slow down, you'd be depositing a wreath on my casket about now."

"It would have to be a small one. I'm saving up for a new easel."

"Hopefully, I'll survive," he said, grinning. "If I do, I stand to be as rich as I've always wanted to be. And that, in case you ain't guessed, is very rich indeed. At any rate, I intend to stay above the ground at least until next Wednesday." Dobkin pointed at his desk calendar. "Until the thirteenth of June."

"My birthday?"

"I have a surprise party planned. I'm telling you about it now, so that if they succeed in bumping me off, you'll know what you missed." Coming around the desk, he took her arm.

"You really aren't kidding about all this, are you?"

"Wish I were, my dear."

"Then why don't you go to the police? Ben and I know a detective on the Brimstone force who—"

"I can't bring the cops in right now," he said. "Soon, but not now."

They started down the red brick steps together. H. J. noticed that the Dahlman limousine was no longer there.

"Even when I strike it rich and depart from this pesthole," Dobkin was assuring her, "they'll keep using your covers."

"I plan to retire from the cover trade fairly soon. But thanks anyway." Her portfolio snagged on something, a branch of one of the decorative shrubs probably, and was jerked from her grip. "Wait a second." She stopped, bending to pick it up.

Dobkin kept going. He started walking across the parking lot, frowning. "Senility is rapidly creeping up on me. I can never remember where I left my damn Mercedes."

H. J. retrieved the portfolio and straightened up.

She heard the roar of an approaching car. A silver Audi was racing in their direction.

For a few seconds she didn't realize what was going to happen. Then she saw that the speeding car was heading straight for Dobkin.

Dobkin saw it, too, and turned to run.

"Lloyd! Look out!"

It hit him. The bumper and the right fender slammed into him.

Dobkin cried out in pain and rose off the ground. He flew up into the gray afternoon, arms flapping, legs twisting in a strange scarecrow way.

He seemed to stay up there longer than he possibly could have.

H. J. was able to see him and at the same time get a quick look at the person driving the car. The driver wore a black knit ski mask and some kind of black jacket.

Dobkin hit the ground, his head smacking hard against the lowest brick step. It made an awful sound.

Crying out, not saying any actual words, H. J. stumbled forward to kneel next to him.

There was blood all over his face, more spilling out of his mouth. "See?" he murmured, glancing up at her. "I told you they were out to get me." Then he let out all his breath and died.

The silver Audi was speeding away up Rivergate Road.

$\triangledown$

3

Like the dwellers in the Alps who don't notice the avalanche until it's carrying their chalet down a steep hillside, Ben Spanner had not the slightest suspicion of what was heading his way. On that gray Tuesday afternoon he had just finished carrying two cardboard cartons of H. J.'s cooking utensils into his spacious white kitchen.

His former wife's collection of pots and pans was a battered and mismatched lot, and he wasn't certain he wanted the stuff to merge with his. Deciding to stow the boxes temporarily in the pantry, he draped a neatly folded dropcloth over them.

He was a sandy-haired man of thirty-seven, almost five foot eight and about thirteen pounds heavier than he thought he ought to be. He returned to his large white living room, sat down on the sofa, and picked up the script he was supposed to be studying.

On this particular radio commercial he was going to play not only Chumley but also one of the crispy English muffins served at the hundreds of My Man Chumley Fish & Chips restaurants around the country.

The basic Chumley voice he'd worked out when he took over the assignment some weeks ago. It was a blend of Ar-

thur Treacher and Ronald Colman, with just a trace of
Claude Rains. But he wasn't yet sure how to do the muffin.

"Well, how about a bumbling Dr. Watson, old boy?" he
asked himself in his Nigel Bruce voice.

Nope, that didn't suggest crispness.

"How about a jolly Prince Philip then, what?"

Too nasal.

The phone on the end table rang.

Dropping the script onto the sofa cushion beside him, he
reached over and grabbed the receiver. "Spanner residence,
don't you know," he said in his Basil Rathbone voice.

"Lord, I don't see how she can stand living with you again.
Silly voices morning, noon, and night."

"Hi, sis," he said in his Archie Andrews voice. "Gee, it's
sure swell to hear from—"

"Ben, please. Address me in your real voice," requested
H. J.'s sister in Westchester.

He kept on as Archie. "Gosh, Betsy, this is my real voice."

With restraint Betsy Hodgins asked, "Is H. J. home?"

He became himself again. "Out to lunch."

Betsy sighed. "Well, maybe this is better," she said, not
sounding exactly certain of that. "I did want to talk to you,
too. It's about Helen Joanne."

"Okay, go ahead, sis." He retrieved the script and scanned
the muffin's dialogue, underlining the key words with a red
porous pen.

"Is my sister really going ahead with this insane thing?"

"Which insane thing? Knowing her, you ought to realize
she's got more than one insane thing in the works at any
given—"

"Moving back in with you full time. That's the specific
insane thing I mean, Ben."

He nodded. "She is, yeah. Should have all her essential
belongings here by the end of the week or thereabout."

Another sigh. "And you are planning to remarry?"

"We haven't decided. But that does seem, to me anyway,
the next logical step, Betts."

"When you two were married before, it wasn't exactly smooth sailing."

"True, but we're both older and wiser. Not to mention richer."

"That's another thing that bothers me," continued his ex-wife's sister. "H. J. tells me she's thinking of giving up her career."

"Not exactly, no. What she is figuring on doing is giving up the paperback covers for a while and trying some gallery painting again," he explained, setting the script aside. "Then this fall she's going to take a couple courses at the New Haven School of Fine Arts."

"She's only thirty-two, a little early for a midlife crisis."

"Thirty-one," he corrected. "Her birthday isn't until—"

"Who's going to pay for all this?"

"She's saved some from her commercial artwork, and she'll probably sell her cottage."

"But with the real estate market the way it is, she may not see any money from that for—"

"On top of which, Betts, I am doing okay these days. Since I landed the My Man Chumley account, my income has gone up to—"

"Oh, I don't like to have people tell me how much they—"

"To five hundred thousand a year. So, if H. J. runs out of her own funds, she still won't—"

"That's going to make her completely dependent on you."

"Listen, she's being doing very well painting book covers. She can always fall back on that if and when she comes to her senses and ditches me."

"And that Chumley business," continued his sister-in-law. "I suppose it's a plum for you, but after all you killed the poor man who used to be Chumley in the commercials, and to me that—"

"Now just a minute, sis," he cut in, angry. "The police shot him. Not me, not H. J. And the poor man was actually a murderer."

"But it was you who got Helen Joanne tangled up with all

those terrible people. Murderers, blackmailers, and—"

"No, *she* got *me* entangled," he corrected. "And, if you'll search through the memories filed in that peabrain of yours, Betsy dear, you'll maybe recall that it is often Helen Joanne who gets those near and dear to her mixed up in various and sundry messes. Now, don't think I'm ungrateful for your interest in me and my humble career, but, dammit, I saved her life. Those bastards were going to kill her and—"

"Yes, all right, Ben, I know. I'm sorry," said Betsy, not sounding especially contrite. "But you can see that it's only natural for me to be concerned about my younger sister. Especially if you take into consideration that she's obviously inherited not only our father's artistic talent but also his tendency to stir up—"

"Whoa, halt," he warned. "I've vowed never to discuss the late Edwin Mavity with anyone."

"Yes, I can understand how you feel, considering how he treated—"

"I have to go now. I'll tell her you phoned. How's Spike?"

"Who?"

"Spike, your husband."

"His name is Buzz."

"Right, that's the one. Give him our best. Bye." He hung up.

He was still leaning back on the sofa, staring at the distant white ceiling, when H. J. let herself in.

She shut the door quietly, stood leaning against it. She was holding a manila envelope to her chest.

He stood, frowning. "What's wrong?"

"I'm afraid," she said faintly, "that I'm involved in another murder."

H. J. was clutching the coffee cup with both hands, both elbows resting on the big butcher block kitchen table. The manila envelope was resting near her right elbow. Setting the cup carefully down, she began, very softly, to sob. "I'm sorry," she murmured as he moved his chair around next to hers. "It's been a very . . . um . . . bizarre day. I spent all afternoon being grilled by your cop buddy, Detective Ryerson. Even when they finally let me head for home—when I started driving up Rivergate, Post Road was shut down and everybody had to make a circumlocutious detour because a truck had overturned and spilled something all over the damn street."

He put an arm gently around her shoulders. "Spilled what?"

"I'm not exactly sure. Either toxic waste or maple syrup. Made a big mess." She picked up her coffee cup, sipped. "Earlier, I almost got killed, too. It was only by chance, I think, that I didn't."

"Tell me what happened."

"Lloyd Dobkin, Ben." She shook her head, sniffling. "He's dead. He was murdered."

"Jesus, we've both know him for years. That's terrible. What happened?"

"A car hit him." H. J. put down her cup but kept both hands tightly clasped around it. "See, Lloyd and I were coming out of the Dahlman Building. About one o'clock, to go to lunch. Then this big silver Audi just came speeding across the parking lot. I'd—I don't know why—dropped my portfolio and I stooped to pick the thing up. Lloyd kept walking for his car. We were going to drive over to Westport to Arnie's and . . . the car just hit him. Hit him very hard and sent him flying into the air. He cracked his head on the steps when he landed. The car kept going and drove on out of there and up Rivergate Road."

"Sounds too deliberate to be a hit-and-run."

"Especially, Ben, since the person driving the car was wearing a ski mask."

"You sure of that?"

"Yes, I saw the driver clearly. Even though I didn't get the license number, I saw who was behind the wheel. Please don't start sounding like your pal Ryerson."

"He's not, Helen Joanne, exactly my close buddy. I appeared, you know, at a police benefit once and did some of my voices. That's how I got to know Ryerson casually. Then

when you and I got mixed up in Rick Dell's murder a couple
of months ago, Ryerson was the one who—"

"When I got you mixed up in the murder, you mean."

"Whatever it was, that mess brought us back together
again."

"You sound like you're saying, 'That's how I caught bu-
bonic plague.' "

"No, I'd say that like this," he explained, and then repeated
her line in his Boris Karloff voice. "Does anybody around the
Dahlman works have any idea why Dobkin was killed?"

"Most of them were reacting pretty hysterically, so they
weren't too coherent." She sipped her coffee again. "Eva tried
to throw herself on his body, which was probably closer than
she'd been to him in months. Then she took me aside to
assure me that even though Lloyd was a first-rate son of a
bitch, she had loved him dearly. That the squabble I'd over-
heard between them just before he got killed was nothing
more than a little spat."

"Was it?"

"I don't know. She turned purple and told him she hoped
he'd die—soon and painfully. But for her maybe that is only
a spat."

"Did you tell Ryerson about their fighting?"

"I gave him a toned-down version," answered H. J.
"Brother Larry was there, too. He broke down and cried. He
was wearing this purple and gold running outfit and blub-
bering about how while he'd been out running the same old
route he runs faithfully every day, why, his dear brother-in-
law was being slaughtered. If he'd been there, he might've
saved him and so on. The implication being that if I hadn't
been a frail woman, I could've pulled Lloyd from the path of
the death car or something."

"That's doubtful, H. J."

"I couldn't help, though, thinking about how my father
died and—"

"You couldn't have prevented that either. Tell me more
about what happened today."

"Old man Dahlman drove up in his limo while they were still taking pictures of the body. He'd been there before and then came back for some reason. He stayed hidden in his car and sent his chauffeur to ask the cops what was going on."

He watched her face. "Do you have any notion about why Lloyd was killed?"

After a few silent seconds she answered, "I do, yes."

"Did you tell Ryerson?"

"Not exactly."

"Not exactly?"

"Not at all, actually." She let go of the cup to push the manila envelope three inches to the right. "Ryerson already thinks I'm a loon. So I kept my theories to myself."

"He doesn't think you're a loon."

"If not a loon, at least a dimwit."

"Possibly a dimwit. Why do you think Dobkin was murdered?"

She said, "Remember last week I mentioned that Lloyd thought somebody was trying to kill him?"

Ben frowned thoughtfully. "Nope."

"I didn't take it very seriously myself, so I didn't dwell on it. It was while we were having dinner at Orlando's restaurant down by the Sound."

"I've forgotten what you said."

"Well, you told me at the time that Dobkin had a great imagination and was continually dramatizing himself. That he was always overflowing with get-rich-quick schemes, and on top of that he suffered from persecution mania."

"Hey, I was pretty eloquent. I wish I'd paid more attention to what I was saying."

"I'm afraid I more or less agreed with you. Worse than that, I told Lloyd I was sure he was exaggerating."

"What forms did the other attempts take? They didn't keep trying to run him down with a car, did they?"

"Actually there had only been one other try when I told you. But there was a second one." She eased the envelope three inches to the left. "Lloyd told me something about that today. Just before the third, and final, attempt."

"What form did the other two take?"

"First time somebody strung a wire across the stairs and he tripped over it in the dark and fell."

"Maybe Eva?"

"He wasn't coming out of his own bedroom at the time. Lloyd fooled around a lot, you know."

"He told me that, but I never exactly believed him."

"He did."

"Which gives Eva another motive besides just not liking him."

"He swore she had nothing to do with it and didn't know where he was that night."

Shrugging, he asked, "And the second try?"

"He was cagier about all the details, at least as to exactly whom he was with. But at another of his women's places," she said, "someone drained his brake fluid, and he came close to having a serious auto accident."

Ben got up and began pacing the wide kitchen. "Yep, those pretty much qualify as earlier attempts to knock him off," he said. "Did he tell you why he thought somebody was out to get him?"

"He was pretty vague, but it had something to do with a discovery. A discovery he'd made within the past few weeks. I got the impression that there were people who didn't want what he knew to become public."

"What sort of discovery are we talking about? A cure for the common cold, perpetual motion?"

"It had to do with a major crime," she replied. "He was planning to write a book about it. He also mentioned there'd definitely be a television show, a docudrama."

"Are we talking about organized crime?"

H. J. shook her head. "I don't think so."

"I'm a man of some means these days." He stopped pacing to frown at her. "This new Chumley deal, coupled with all the other commercial voice stuff I do, will bring in around half a million a year for a while. So there's no problem about your quitting the romance covers and concentrating on serious painting again. Therefore, there's no need to pursue this, as I suspect you're contemplating, in the hope that you'll figure out how Dobkin was planning to make big money and then make some for yourself. Keep in mind, Helen Joanne, the important fact that he didn't get rich, he just got dead."

"I know, I know. He practically died in my arms."

"Hold it. Dobkin didn't deliver some kind of dying message, did he?"

"No, he only said, 'I told you they were trying to kill me.' And I'd just been kidding him about how he was probably imagining things."

"That's like the old joke."

"This isn't the proper time for jokes, old or otherwise."

"Wife drags her husband to the doctor and says, 'My husband is terribly sick. You've got to do something to help him.' The doctor examines the guy, but he assures her there's nothing wrong with him at all. Since he's also something of a psychiatrist, he tells her, 'Ma'am, it's all in his mind. Your husband isn't actually sick. He only thinks he's sick.' Two weeks later on the street he sees her again and asks, 'How's your husband?' She answers, 'Now he thinks he's dead.' "

"That must be another of those jokes you're always saying are profound rather than funny."

"It fits the situation. Nobody apparently believed Dobkin was on the brink of being killed, but he was," said Ben. "He's dead and gone. And you could be, too, if you persist in poking into this."

H. J. slid the envelope in front of her. "I know that since we'll be living together again, I really won't have any monetary worries, because you'll be there to bail me out if need be," she said. "It's important to me, though, that you won't have to finance me and that whatever I do and whatever our marital status, I can pay my own way."

"Okay, but there are all sorts of other ways of making

money. We don't know exactly what Dobkin was on to, but
it's damn certain it's something that can get people killed
and—"

"There's more to this than money, Ben. Lloyd was a friend
and I'd like to find out who killed him. The way he died does
remind me of my father's death and—"

"It isn't rational to compare a—"

"I'm not claiming to be exactly rational. I'm only telling
you how I feel and what I'd like to do," she said, opening the
manila envelope. "Lloyd gave me this today. I didn't look at
it at the time, just popped it into my portfolio. He told me
to look after it, as a sort of hole card for him. In case someone
found his files."

"His files on what?"

"That's another of the things he didn't confide in me."
From the envelope she drew an eight-by-ten color photograph. "I didn't look at this until after I got clear of the
Dahlman Building. Doesn't convey much to me, but maybe
you can figure something."

Ben took the photo from her. "I'll be jinged," he muttered
in his New England rustic voice.

He found himself holding a blow-up of a photo of a young
woman's backside. On her left buttock was a small birthmark that looked exactly like a tiny black butterfly. He
turned the picture over, but there was nothing written on
the reverse.

"She's got a cute ass, whoever she is," he said finally. "But
I haven't any notion what this means or why Dobkin gave
it to you."

$\triangledown$

4

THUNDER RUMBLED. THE WINDOWS of the master bedroom rattled, and heavy rain commenced hitting against the panes.

Ben sat suddenly upright, half awake. "They stole the butterfly!" he shouted as the last of his nightmare faded away.

Gradually he became fully awake. He shook his head a few times, took a slow careful breath in and out. Reaching over, he gave H. J. a reassuring pat on her backside. Her rear end felt oddly saggy and insubstantial.

Lightning crackled outside, and the big room was filled for a few seconds with silky blue light. Ben discovered that he'd been consoling a wadded up tangle of blankets. H. J. wasn't in bed.

After switching on the bedside lamp, he stumbled out of bed and stood for a moment on the carpet. "There's something I have to tell her," he said, trying to remember exactly what it was. "About the butterfly birthmark, wasn't it?"

He wandered over to the open doorway. As always he'd been sleeping in a pajama top and shorts.

Moving out into the long dark upstairs hall, he called out, "H. J.?"

There was no response.

The night rain thumped on the skylights.

Ben ventured farther along the hall, heading for the stairway. "Hey! Helen Joanne?"

"Down here. Quit yowling."

"I happen to be master of this manse." He clicked on the stair lights and went trotting down to the living room. "So I have full yowling privileges."

He found his erstwhile wife sitting on the sofa, legs tucked under her, studying the photo Dobkin had entrusted to her. H. J. was wearing one of his old blue button-down shirts and nothing else. "Couldn't sleep," she explained, holding the picture at arm's length and squinting at it.

"Just before I dozed off, I think something crossed my mind." He ambled over and sat close beside her. "Then I must've dreamt about it."

"Is that what you were hollering about just now?"

Ben pointed at the birthmark on the mystery woman's left buttock. "I was dreaming about people stealing butterflies," he recalled, frowning. "Wait a minute, wait."

"Are you on the verge of having a vision?"

"They stole the butterfly. Sure, right. That's it." Standing up, bouncing a couple times on the balls of his feet, he began pacing.

She nodded at his legs. "Were you that shaggy back when we were married?"

"Sure. Macho men are always hairy."

"From the waist down you look like the Wolfman."

"You ought to see me during the full moon," he said in his Lon Chaney, Jr. voice. Then he stopped still, nodding with satisfaction. "What I've been trying to remember is a kidnapping."

"Whose?"

"Her. The girl with the butterfly on her backside. They kidnapped her."

"Feminists would prefer that you call her a young woman."

"No, no. This was twenty years or more ago. She was a little girl, no more than two or three. It's a famous case."

"What's her name?"

"I can't remember."

"So much for fame."

"Yeah, but it's one of the cases Dobkin wrote up in that book of his, the one he gave you a copy of. *Great American Kidnappings*," he told her. "As I was falling asleep, I must've remembered the picture of that little girl's rear end in Dobkin's book. Where'd you put it?"

She got up, forehead furrowing. "You're saying that's who this is?" She waved the photograph back and forth, as though she were drying it off. "This is the kidnap victim grown up?"

"We can compare the two birthmarks, soon as you locate the book. He gave it to you only a few weeks ago."

She sat. "Shit," she said. "I don't know where it is, Ben."

He crossed over to his wall-high bookcases. "I remember browsing through it right after Dobkin presented it to you. I left it sitting on that end table."

"That's always been a problem with you, leaving stuff lying around."

"You must've stuck it on a shelf someplace. You have a compulsion about tidying up."

H. J. thought. "I remember," she said finally, brightening. "I took it over to my place and stuck it on a shelf in my studio."

"Why?"

"In case Lloyd visited me there while I was batting out a godawful Gossamer Library job," she replied. "I've been trying to get him to raise the price per cover by at least another five hundred dollars."

"That might've done it. If I were an author, I'd give out five hundred to anybody who had one of my books prominently displayed."

"We've got to get hold of that book."

"Sure, first thing in the morning."

"No. Right now, tonight."

"You want to go out in the middle of the night, during a violent thunderstorm?"

She nodded emphatically before running toward the staircase. "This is going to help us solve Lloyd's murder," she said, starting up the stairs to dress. "And there's also probably a lot of money to be made out of all this."

The night rain came rushing toward the car, slamming the windshield.

H. J., who was sitting up very straight in the passenger seat, asked, "What's that odd muttering noise the engine's making?"

"That's not the car." Ben clutched the steering wheel more tightly as he guided the car along the rainswept lane. "That's me."

"Oh, so?"

"I was cursing my fate."

"A favorite hobby of yours, as I recall."

He slowed the car as he noticed a large tree branch had fallen across the road ahead. There was just enough room to skirt it. "Trees are being felled by the powerful forces of nature," he said in his plummy documentary voice, "yet our intrepid wayfarers press on. There are those who'd call them foolhardy . . . and they'd be absolutely right."

"Don't be such a grump. This is fun. C'mon, admit it."

"Nope. Shooting the rapids in a canoe might be fun, going over Niagara Falls in a keg might be fun. But driving through a monsoon in the wee hours of the morning is not fun."

She shrugged her left shoulder. "I've been thinking about what must have happened," she said. "Somebody, purely by chance, sent in some pictures of this young lady to *Bare*. I'd guess that it was to their 'My Best Girl' section, which is, you know, open to amateur models and photographers."

"And Lloyd recognized the birthmark."

"If you're right about their being similar, yes."

"Then what would he have done?"

"I'm not certain. Myself, after getting very excited, I'd try to contact the young woman or the person who took her picture and submitted them. I wouldn't let on I thought she was a missing heiress, but I'd find out all I could about her."

"We don't know she's a missing heiress. She could be a missing pauper."

"Lloyd hinted there was a lot of money tied up with what he was involved in," she said. "I wish you could remember more about that chapter in his darn book."

"I never really read it. I just skimmed through the book, looking mostly at the pictures."

"I'm pretty sure that what we've got here, Ben, is one of those situations where the kidnapping victim never showed up again," she said. "But she wasn't killed, and now, probably unaware of who she really is, she turns up. There was a movie on TV a while back with that plot."

"There often is, Helen Joanne. I wouldn't, though, set my heart on finding a long-lost heiress or a missing princess."

"But she's got to be somebody important. Otherwise Lloyd wouldn't have become so enthusiastic."

"The guy had an unlimited capacity for enthusiasm."

"You're just being critical of him because he was an optimist and you aren't."

"I am, too, an optimist. Would a pessimist risk his life on these rustic byways at the height of a typhoon?"

"You just," she observed, "drove past my turn."

H. J. caught hold of his arm. "Don't get out of the car yet," she cautioned quietly.

He'd just parked in the driveway in front of her cottage and turned off the motor. "Something wrong?"

She was slightly hunched, staring out through the hard-falling rain at her house. "I always leave a night-light on in my studio to make burglars think I'm home when I'm really not."

"You'd have to be an exceptionally dumb burglar to—"

"The light isn't on now."

He was looking out toward the small shingled house. "Yeah, the place is as dark as a tomb . . . and other spooky locations I wouldn't care to enter."

"Could be just that the bulb burned out."

"Could be, but—"

"Lately people seem to think they can trash my lodgings whenever they please," she said angrily. "Let's go in and confront the bastards."

"Hold on," he advised, reaching across to open the glove compartment. "I've been carrying a flashlight, since we seem to do so much night work."

"You can't shoot anybody with that."

"Nevertheless. You stick here and I'll circle the house, peep in at the windows to determine if—"

"I'm lighter on my feet than you are." She took the flash from his grasp.

Ben grabbed it back and in so doing bumped against the horn with his elbow.

Two loud blaring hoots shot out across the rainy night.

H. J. sank bank. "Well, if anybody's still prowling in there, that'll surely send them scooting."

"Yeah, it will." Grinning, Ben hit the horn twice again. "Since you don't have any near neighbors, this won't wake anybody. Although maybe nobody's asleep in Brimstone tonight anyway. They're probably all out looting, pillaging, or hunting for missing heirs."

"No one has come out of the house." She opened her door and stepped out into the rainy darkness. "We can risk a look."

Getting out, Ben joined her on the gravel drive. Hand in hand, they ran up to the front door of the dark cottage.

H. J. lifted the keys out of her jacket pocket. "Can somebody be after that photo already?"

"Seems like a good possibility."

The door swung open. H. J. hesitated, then crossed into the house. She sneezed three times.

"You okay?" Ben stepped ahead into the darkness.

"Something in the air made me sneeze."

"I don't smell anything. What?"

She sniffed. "Not sure. It seems to be gone now. I can't smell it anymore."

"Well, let's look around." He moved a few feet over, located the light switch and flicked on the lights.

"Damn," commented H. J. forlornly.

Her living room had been very thoroughly and rapidly ransacked.

$\triangledown$

5

BEN RETURNED FROM THE bedroom of the cottage. "Nobody lurking in there either," he announced. "The house is absolutely free of—"

"Did you look under the bed?"

"You've got a futon, remember? Only a very slim—"

"Okay, let's find that book." H. J. went striding toward her studio.

"I don't know how much entertaining you did on that futon," he observed, following her. "It looks about three degrees less comfortable than a bed of nails. Your boyfriends must've been saying 'Ouch! Ow! Yikes!' from dusk till—"

"Help me find Lloyd's book. It's got a red dust jacket." She halted before her bookcases. Most of the books had been pulled off the shelves and were strewn about on the floor.

Ben crossed to the telephone on the taboret. "First we'll call the police." He reached for the receiver.

She ran over to his side, slapping her hand over his. "I've had my minimum daily requirement of police for today, thanks," she informed her onetime spouse. "The last thing I want to do is explain to Detective Ryerson why thugs tossed my place."

"We're probably dealing with the same folks who killed

Dobkin," he reminded her. "They must have been looking for that photo." He nodded at her shoulder bag.

"Maybe." She kept her hand pressed down over his.

"Or worse, H. J., they may think he also gave you his mysterious files. Since they didn't find anything here tonight, they'll—"

"Suppose all that is absolutely true. What the heck is Ryerson going to do?"

"Well, first off he'll note the fact that you've been burgled. Then he and his crew will sift the cottage for clues."

She made a rude noise. "And find nothing," she said. "C'mon, Ben, burglars are smart. They wear gloves and they long ago quit dropping matchbooks from the Kit Kat Klub where gumshoes can find them."

"Also, you're going to need protection."

"Really? And is Ryerson going to move in with us and spend his nights camped outside the bedroom with a shotgun in his lap?"

"Probably not, no. But what normal, rational people are supposed to do in a situation like this is follow a—"

"What we, on the other hand, are going to do is exactly what we did last time."

"Last time you ended up getting kidnapped, tortured, and nearly terminated."

"You know what I mean. Quit being so negative. What we have to do is look out for ourselves."

"*Ourselves?* Hellsfire, I always start out an innocent bystander and somehow—no doubt because I'm traveling under a curse—somehow it always ends up that *we* are in trouble."

"You can desert right now, scamper right off the sinking ship. I don't give a fiddler's damn."

"Tinker's."

"Huh?"

"A tinker's damn. That's what people don't give."

"Just go home if you want, pull the quilt over your melon-shaped head. I'll carry on alone."

"Hey, I'm not going to abandon you. I'm just trying to point out the sensible thing to—"

"Kvetching is what you're doing, as is your wont."

"Really, H. J., we should alert the cops."

"No, what we should do is solve Lloyd's murder." Her fingers tightened over his. "That's the only way we can be certain the gang that wrecked my cottage will be locked away."

"Playing detective isn't the smartest, or safest, thing to do."

"Worked before."

"More or less."

"All right, we'll compromise," suggested H. J. "We'll work on this, oh, for a couple of days or so. If we don't come up with anything, then we'll go, hand in hand, I promise, to Detective Ryerson."

"In, oh, a couple of days, we may both be stretched out in some cozy funeral parlor."

"A sourpuss, true, might well look at things that way," she admitted. "But I think we make a good team."

In his old-time radio announcer voice he said, "And now it's time once again for Mr. and Mrs. North. In tonight's thrilling episode lovely scatterbrained H. J. Mavity moves even further from reality, while her long-suffering husband finds himself waist deep in—"

"*Former* husband."

"A slip, excuse it. The point, however, is that—"

"Please, let's try it my way." She looked hopefully at him. "No police. Not yet anyway."

Giving up, he lifted his hand away from the phone. "Okay." In his stern judge voice he added, "And may God have mercy on our souls."

H. J. found the book.

It was in a spill of books the ransacker had left dumped near a foot of the easel.

"Bingo," she announced, scooping up *Great American*

Kidnappings and sitting down cross-legged on the mat rug, "here it is."

As Ben sat down next to her, she handed him Dobkin's book. "It was one of the earlier chapters," he said, thumbing rapidly but carefully through the pages. "Yes sir, here's the picture I was thinking of."

She leaned closer. "Does look similar, doesn't it?"

The photo illustration showed a blond baby girl of about a year and a half lying on a flowered blanket. She was stretched out on her stomach, and an arrow had been drawn in pointing to the birthmark on her buttock.

" 'The distinctive butterfly birthmark of the missing Timberlake baby,' " read Ben. "Of course, I should have remembered—this is Sue Ellen Timberlake. Got a magnifying glass?"

"Someplace." Rising up, H. J. rummaged in the scatter of stuff atop the taboret. "Here." She tossed him a small reading glass. From her shoulder bag she took the photograph that Lloyd Dobkin had entrusted to her.

Ben was studying the baby's bottom through the lens. "Let's compare this with the Best Girl."

"Are they the same?" She sat, holding the color blowup next to the book page.

"Sure seems to be, taking into consideration that more than twenty years have passed between photo sessions."

Squinting at the page, H. J. nodded. "Sure, it's the same, identical tush," she said. "Didn't you do a radio spot for one of the Timberlake products?"

"Several." He was continuing to compare the birthmarks. "Timberlake, Inc., manufactures Sudz, Bubblez, Kleenz, Scrubz, and several other products that help to keep this great nation of ours clean and sparkling. The Forman & McCay agency, for whom I now do the Chumley stuff, also handles the Sudz account. That alone bills $87 million per year. Matter of fact, the last batch of radio commercials I did for Sudz, wherein I portrayed a dirty argyle sock, are up for an—"

"And who exactly is Sue Ellen Timberlake?" She took the book away from him. " 'Only child of the widowed Anson Timberlake . . . inventive genius who founded Timberlake, Inc. . . . amassed estate estimated at $270 million . . . estate and the controlling interest in the company went to the two children of his only brother at the time of his death in 1980.' Gosh.

"One of the two heirs is Don T. Timberlake, who is what is known, technically, as a first-class prick. One of his homes is near here over in Southport."

Ben took the book back. "The other is his sister, Laura Timberlake Barks, who resides in Chicago and the Bahamas. It's likely though, that Laura will be in Manhattan for—"

"Suppose Sue Ellen really is alive?" H. J. tapped the color photo with her forefinger. "She'd be worth a heck of a lot of money."

"True," he agreed.

"It's possible the Timberlakes wouldn't want her found."

"Also true," said Ben.

▽

6

THE RAIN HAD SOFTENED to a drizzle by dawn; the new morning was fuzzy and gray. The small, rutted parking lot alongside Fagin's Diner on Post Road in Westport was even bleaker than usual, and next to the rusted green Dumpster crouched a forlorn calico cat who was suffering from a head cold.

H. J. turned up the collar of her tan windbreaker. "How did you come to pick Fagin's as a hangout in the first place?"

As they climbed the brick steps to the door, Ben replied, "I've repressed all memory of that."

Fagin himself, a small fifty-five-year-old man with a pale, stubbly face, was hunched in the middle of the center aisle. "Okay, okay, you mothering horsefly, light somewhere." He clutched a spatula in his right hand.

Ben and H. J. eased around the crouching proprietor and headed for a rear booth, where their friend Joe Sankowitz was seated.

"Fresh from the motel, huh, Spanner?" called Fagin, his narrowed eyes on the circling fly.

"You're looking especially dapper this morning, Fagin," Ben said. "Are you shaving every three days now instead of every four?"

Fagin lunged at the fly, swinging the greasy spatula and

whapping a spot on the counter. "Missed. Shit."

Sankowitz was a lean, dark man in his early forties. He had a copy of the *Brimstone Pilot* spread out before him. "You folks look like you've been up to no good," he observed. "Are you dragging him into another morass of mystery and intrigue, Helen?"

H. J. smiled innocently. "Just because we're up with the lark and happened to drop in to this pesthole for coffee, that's no reason to assume—"

"I bet the lark was murdered. Is there a lot of money involved?"

"Matter of fact," said Ben, sliding in opposite him, "we are sort of mixed up in something, Joe."

Their cartoonist friend nodded, grinning. He poked at the front page of the folded newspaper. "Does it maybe have something to do with the murder of Lloyd Dobkin?" he asked them. "It says here H. J. was the leading witness."

"It does, yep." Reaching across the tabletop, Ben borrowed the newspaper.

"You knew Lloyd, didn't you?" H. J. asked.

Sankowitz said, "In my earlier, struggling days, prior to becoming the darling of *The New Yorker,* I used to sell gag cartoons to *Bare.* I still saw Lloyd for lunch now and then. I even dropped in at the Dahlman Building and risked getting bonked by whatever Eva was hurling at him that day."

"Seeing the car bearing down on him and not being able to do anything," said H. J., "was pretty terrible."

"There are a lot of things in life you can't do anything about," said the cartoonist. "It's too bad, but that seems to be one of the ground rules. Best thing you can do, Helen, is to forget that—"

"The police found the Audi that ran him down," said Ben, who'd been reading the story.

"Probably stolen," guessed H. J.

A thin waitress appeared and set down two more cups of coffee. "Avoid the sausage," she warned in a side-of-the-mouth whisper before departing.

Ben said, "Yeah, it was stolen from a dentist in Westport. Cops found it abandoned on a road in that nature preserve about a half mile up from the Dahlman Building. No prints, no clues. At least not any they're talking about."

H. J. took a tentative sip of her coffee. "Uck. How can you guys drink this stuff?"

"Well, I figure anything that tastes this bad," explained Sankowitz, "must be good for you."

"Describes you here as 'a lovely redheaded commercial artist,' " Ben told her.

She took the paper from him. "No color sense. Auburn isn't red."

"Be thankful they at least got the lovely part right," advised Ben.

"Oh, here's a story about the spill," she said, pointing to it. "The stuff was molasses and not toxic sludge. A truck rolled over and burst just after 12:40 P.M. That was just minutes after I drove by on my way to meet Lloyd."

Sankowitz said, "Took them hours to clean it up. Good thing it wasn't this part of Post Road or there'd be molasses in all of Fagin's syrup pitchers this morning."

"That's like the joke about the spillover in the chocolate factory," said Ben.

"No more parables," requested H. J., leaning back wearily.

The cartoonist asked, "Are there perhaps things you know that the paper doesn't?"

"There are things we know," answered Ben, "that even the police don't know."

"You'd better tell them," he advised.

H. J. assured him, "Oh, we're going to."

"But first?"

"First we have to do a little more investigating."

"You're dealing with somebody who steals cars to use as murder weapons," he reminded them. "Very few people with that personality trait take kindly to amateur sleuths—even lovely redheaded ones."

"Lloyd just wasn't my editor, you know. He was my friend,

and I think I owe it to his memory to help find out who did this to him."

"Possibly there are a few people I'd risk life and limb for," said Sankowitz. "But there's not one editor on that list."

"I feel differently," she told him, "obviously."

"How much money is involved?"

"Money has absolutely nothing to do with it," she insisted. "Well, let me clarify that. Money is not the *primary* motivation."

"It's probably a very strong contender for second place, though."

Ben said, "We think Lloyd was on to something big."

"Lloyd continually believed he was on to something important and lucrative," their friend pointed out. "Far as I know, however, none of his discoveries or schemes ever paid off."

"This may have been the exception," said H. J.

A frown touched the cartoonist's face. "And that's tied in with his getting killed?"

"We think so."

"Show him the picture," suggested Ben.

She reached into her shoulder bag. "Lloyd gave this to me yesterday."

"Aha!" cried Fagin. "Got you at last, you little bastard!" After scraping the remains of the fly off the counter with the side of the spatula, he withdrew to the kitchen.

"What the hell is this?" Sankowitz was eyeing the blowup.

"Explain it to him." H. J. took back the picture, returned it to the envelope, and put them away.

"Okay, here's what we've found out." Ben told him what H. J. had witnessed, what they'd been up to since last night, and the conclusions they'd come to.

When Ben finished, Sankowitz asked, "And where is this heiress now?"

"That's one of the things we don't know yet," admitted H. J. "But we're going to find her."

"What'll you do if you locate the woman?"

"Talk to her, tell her she's the long-lost Timberlake baby."

"At which point she hands you a handsome reward, huh?"

"Is that such an improbable scenario, Joseph? If somebody came and told me I had a legitimate right to a ton of money, I'd sure as heck be grateful."

Sankowitz drank some of his vile coffee. "Suppose this whole business was just another of Lloyd's half-assed schemes?"

"Meaning?"

"Meaning maybe he hired some skin model, tattooed a butterfly on her butt, and was planning to pass her off as—"

"What the heck would that gain him? Her fingerprints, her footprints, her blood type—all that's on file someplace."

"You can get a whole stewpot of national publicity before anybody gets to the fingerprinting stage." Sankowitz framed a headline in the air. "*Bare* editor finds missing heiress. Sex mag solves twenty-year-old mystery. See latest issue of *Bare* for details."

H. J. rested both elbows on the table. "People don't usually kill you just for planning a hoax."

"Who says his death had a damn thing to do with the Timberlake baby? Lloyd was a world class philanderer," he pointed out. "An irate husband could have knocked the guy off. I've run into a few of those myself, and some of them can get pretty violent over being cuckolded. Or, which also makes considerable sense, maybe Eva got tired of his sleeping around and decided to bench him permanently. Or perhaps old man Dahlman, dismayed at the way Lloyd was so flamboyantly unfaithful to his only daughter, called on a couple of his old underworld cronies to—"

"Maybe little green weirdos from Mars killed him to keep him from telling where their flying saucer was parked," cut in H. J., annoyed. "C'mon, Joe. Lloyd gave me this photograph, he told me he was on to a big story *and* that there'd been attempts on his life. Then—*bam!*—he's killed."

"Just because two things *seem* to be linked, it doesn't mean they actually are," Sankowitz persisted. "Let the police really find out what the truth is." He glanced over at Ben. "Are you buying all this?"

"I accept the notion that Lloyd had discovered something important," he said. "Further, somebody really has been trying to find his files. Now, maybe he was killed for an entirely different reason—which I sort of doubt—but I still think he'd found the Timberlake girl."

"Tulip mania," muttered the cartoonist.

"Eh?"

"When a delusion starts rolling, lots of otherwise rational people hop aboard."

"Hey," called Fagin from the depths of his kitchen, "this isn't the goddamn Christian Science Reading Room. Chow down or ship out."

"Hotcakes," called Sankowitz.

"Same," called Ben.

"Pass," said H. J.

$\triangledown$

7

H.J. WAS DRIVING them home. "Well, of course you have stomach cramps," she told her erstwhile husband. "Anyone who'd willingly eat at Fagin's has to expect that."

"You still haven't comprehended the idea of Fagin's." Ben was hunched in the passenger seat, gazing absently out into the gray morning. "The food is vile, certainly, and so is Fagin. The thing is, that diner has become a hangout, a habitual place to go."

"Teenage boys need hangouts, not old coots like you and Joe."

He reached into her shoulder bag, located the roll of Pepto-Bismol tablets and availed himself of another one. "Fagin's is the equivalent of a gentlemen's club, minus the armchairs."

"Speaking of Joe, he sure has a negative attitude." She guided the car onto the road that led to his house.

"Practical is what it is."

"Hooey."

"Could be he's right, H. J. Maybe this time we ought to—"

"*I'm* going to find Sue Ellen Timberlake. You can sit around and mope, but—"

"Okay, okay. So what's our first move?"

"We have to get hold of Lloyd's files on this business," she said. "He had other photographs of the woman, pictures that must show more than just her fanny. There should also be addresses and phone numbers, maybe hers and certainly those of the nitwit who submitted the pictures to *Bare*. And probably he had notes on what he had done thus far and how he was planning to proceed. Right now we don't even know if he'd contacted her."

"Not likely he'd leave that stuff at his office, is it?"

"No, I doubt he'd leave anything important there."

"Unless he was using the purloined letter dodge."

"Nope, that wouldn't work with dear Eva, since she's the kind who looks in all the obvious places first. I'm sure she snooped around his office on a regular basis."

"Then he probably wouldn't have left the stuff around home either."

"Not likely, Ben, though we'll have to check out his office at the Dahlman Building and his den at home to be absolutely sure," she said. "Lloyd hated computers and refused to use one, so it's not likely he stored anything *in* one."

"Then where would he stash important material? Maybe with one of his lady friends?"

"Yeah, that's my notion. I think we better start with Micki and Terri first. Do you happen to know their last names?"

"Micki Wilder, former flight attendant, married. Resides in nearby Wilton."

"How do you know all that?"

"With you Lloyd was discreet about his ladies. With guys he sometimes bragged."

"And Terri, who's she?"

"Terri Walters, but she left Connecticut about a month ago to take a job as a librarian in Seattle."

"Seattle's an unlikely place for Lloyd to keep the stuff."

"Wait a minute. He recently started a new romance."

"With whom?"

"Joe mentioned it the other day, expressing surprise that this particular lady would go within a hundred feet of Lloyd. Alicia Bertillion."

"The children's book illustrator? The lady who won a bunch of medals for *Tammy the Turtle?*"

"That Alicia Bertillion, yes. She also wrote and illustrated *Tammy the Turtle's Picnic*. Lives on a high hill over in Redding Ridge."

"She must be the one he was leaving when his brakes went out."

"Reminds me about the old joke about the eunuch who guarded the harem. Seems—"

"We're home," announced H. J., halting the car in the gravel drive.

"Might as well put it in the garage."

"We'll be going out again soon."

"Aw, Helen Joanne," he said in his Wallace Beery voice. "I don't intend to leave home until I do some serious sleeping. It's been several days, feels like, since—"

"Notice our front door." She slid out of the parked car.

"Oh, Christ." He jumped free and started running for the steps.

The heavy wooden door was a good two feet open.

H. J. bent and gathered up another spill of books. "You ought to seriously consider donating most of these to some charitable book fair."

"That's covered in my will, yes, but right now let's just get the damn things back on the shelves. I'd like to be ready for the next wave of burglars."

"You're never going to read them all."

"In my declining years, which may be arriving sooner than I anticipated, thanks to you, I plan to spend a good deal of my time in an easy chair with a good book." He returned another dozen assorted volumes to his living-room shelves.

"I'm sorry they ransacked your place, too," said H. J. "But, since they were obviously looking for whatever Lloyd may've given me, including photos and files, they didn't take anything and the damage isn't all that—"

"During the three years we were apart I wasn't burgled,

looted, or trashed," he said. "Not once."

"Well, neither was I. It's only been recently I started getting tangled up in stuff like this." She reshelved more books.
"But this definitely does prove that Lloyd really was on to
something important."

"I was convinced of that soon as we found out they'd
searched your humble cottage," he said. "This latest dem-
onstration wasn't actually necessary."

She sat on the arm of the sofa, crossing her legs. "Maybe
this second raid proves something else," she said thoughtfully.

Ben said, "You mean that whoever conducted these little
searches has to be familiar with our current life-style?"

H. J. nodded. "Yes, right. They didn't find what they
wanted at my cottage, so they came here next," she said. "So
it has to be somebody who knows we're getting back together
and that I hang out at both addresses."

"Yeah, that might narrow the field of suspects down," he
agreed. "But quite a few people know about us."

"It hasn't been on CNN or in Liz Smith's column. So I
think—"

"Suppose they're searching everybody Lloyd might have
given his files to? I was a chum of his, too," he said. "That
way I'd be on their list even if they didn't know you were—"

"We have got to find his files first, Ben." She stood up.
"And soon."

"I would like to have at least a short nap before—"

The phone rang.

H. J. answered. "Mavity-Spanner residence."

"I don't even get top billing in my own house no more,"
Ben complained in his Rodney Dangerfield voice.

"Hush."

"Is that you, Helen, dear? I tried your cottage and then
thought I might catch you at Ben's."

"Yes, it's me, Eva." Glancing at Ben, she let her eyebrows
climb. "Let me mention again how sad we are about—"

"Yes, yes, dear, everybody is," cut in Dobkin's widow. "But

NOW HE THINKS HE'S DEAD

I honestly believe poor Lloyd would want us to carry on. As a sort of memorial to his memory."

"*Bare* isn't the sort of memorial I personally—"

"Would it be possible for you to drop in around two or so?"

"I suppose so. At your home, you mean?"

"No, I'm at the office," replied Eva. "I need to talk to you about the *Love's Claimant* cover."

"Lloyd already okayed my rough."

"Yes, I know, and I imagine the poor dear man showed, as always, excellent taste," continued Eva. "But now that I'm going to have to oversee our Regency romance line, I feel I should be on top of what's going on. Don't you?"

"Okay, sure. I'll bring over the rough. Is two-thirty okay?"

"Yes, if that's convenient for you, dear."

"I'll see you then. Oh, and when is the funeral going to be?"

"We haven't scheduled it yet. The police are still—well, we'll be letting all Lloyd's many friends know. And there'll be a notice in the *Pilot*."

Hanging up, H. J. said, "That was the grieving widow."

"So I deduced. She going to futz up your cover?"

"More than likely." H. J. looked down at the answering machine. "Oh, you have a message." She punched the play button.

"I hope you're not off on a binge or otherwise unavailable," said Willis McCay of the Forman & McCay advertising agency. "I know you weren't planning to attend the awards luncheon today, old buddy, but I just heard something that makes me think you ought to. Call me soon as you can. As a bonus, I can maybe get you seated next to the gorgeous Laura Timberlake Barks, who is in town for the gala occasion. Bye."

"What awards luncheon today?" asked H. J.

"Some half-wit ad group is giving out trophies for the alleged best radio spots of the year."

"And you're in line for one?"

"Yes, dear. I tried to tell you several times, because it's for those Sudz commercials I did where I play the dirty sock. Since Timberlake owns—"

"You certainly never mentioned any such thing."

In his Raymond Burr voice he said, "If you'll consult the transcript of our conversations over the past twenty-four hours, you'll note that I did indeed."

"If you had mentioned that you'd have an opportunity to pump one of the Timberlake heirs, *and* possibly pick up yet another ugly doodad to clutter this place, I wouldn't have missed that," she insisted. "Now, if you can cease being silly for a minute, let's—"

"Cease being silly? Cease being silly?" he exclaimed in his Sylvester the Cat voice. "Why, suffering—"

"Can McCay really seat you next to her?"

"Probably, if I go. But I'd much rather stay here and snooze."

"Plenty of time to snooze later. You have to attend that lunch."

"You figure I can just lean close to the lady and inquire, 'Say, hon, did you and your putz of a brother knock off Lloyd Dobkin to keep him from revealing who the long-lost Timberlake baby is?' "

"You'll have to be a shade more subtle than that obviously."

"May I can just hum a few bars of 'Poor Butterfly' and see if she turns deathly pale."

"You ought to be able to learn something, Ben, just by talking to her," said H. J., annoyed. "What's the name of this half-wit award anyway?"

"The Paul."

"The Paul? What sort of dippy name is that?"

"Named in honor of Paul Frees, one of the great voice men of yesteryear."

"I suppose that's better than calling the thing the Ben," she said. "Okay, you best phone McCay right away and tell him you're coming. Then you have to get ready and catch a train to Manhattan."

"Only the other day, Helen Joanne, I was reading a piece in the respected *New York Times*. It pointed out that walking in your sleep can be harmful. I'd better stay—"

"We don't have any more time for dawdling." She grabbed up the phone. "I'll get McCay for you."

"Another thing—it's not safe to leave you alone. In case these guys come back."

"I'm sure they're off ransacking other locations by now." To the phone she said, "Mr. McCay, please. This is Ben Spanner's private secretary."

"Are you going to see Eva?"

"You bet I am. It gives me an excuse to poke around Lloyd's office and other nooks and crannies of the Dahlman Building."

"Okay, but please don't go calling on any of Lloyd's old flames until I get back." He took the phone.

"You have my word," she promised sweetly.

$\triangledown$

8

H.J. LEFT THE HOUSE approximately six minutes after Ben did. He'd headed for the Westport station to catch the 11:33 train into New York City.

Restless, convinced she wouldn't be able to nap between then and her meeting with the widow Dobkin, she'd looked up Micki Wilder in the Wilton section of their phone book. Earl and Micki Wilder resided at 232 Mott Lane.

H. J. was pretty sure she knew where that was.

Ben had mentioned that the young woman was a former stewardess. That should mean she'd retired from the workplace and might be found at home during the day.

H. J. didn't want to risk scaring Lloyd's girlfriend by phoning first.

Though the rain had stopped, the day was still gray and the sunlight thin.

"You did promise him you wouldn't call on any of these women alone," she reminded herself as she entered the garage.

Yes, but Ben tended to be overprotective. That was one of the things that had caused their marriage to fall apart the first time.

"But we're not married this go-round, only living together." She climbed into her car, which she kept in his garage these days. "And, anyway, there's nothing especially dangerous about just calling on one of Lloyd's nitwit lady friends. In broad daylight after all."

She backed along the driveway toward the tree-lined road. "Of course, I'll fill him in on everything I've done. He's not likely to be ticked off. Especially if I find out something important."

And she was certain that she would.

Ben stood on the station platform, taking frequent swigs from the cup of black coffee he'd purchased at the café across the way. The stuff tasted a lot better than the bitter brew Fagin tried to pass off as coffee, but it wasn't contributing much toward keeping him awake and alert.

The other commuters scattered along the platform all looked wider awake than he did. Well, by 11:21 in the morning most decent folk were awake. After yawning twice, he drank more coffee.

A heavyset woman in shorts was assuring a heavyset man in shorts, "You're going to like it, Henry."

"I didn't like the novel."

"This is a *musical*."

"Even if they yodel, I'm not going to like it."

At the nearby phone a slim young man in an expensive business suit was saying, "Now he insists he has to have *more* than two mill."

Suddenly a dense cloud of the scents of pine, leather, and musk engulfed Ben. Narrowing an eye, he looked to his left and saw large Larry Dahlman approaching.

"I suppose you heard all about it from H. J.?" Larry inquired, holding out his hand.

Ben shook hands, then absently wiped his palm on the side of his coat. "Yeah. I'm sorry about Lloyd."

"I hear—perhaps this is none of my business—that you and H. J. are together again."

"We are."

"She's a very attractive woman."

"She is."

"And exceptionally bright and witty."

"That, too."

"I'm very fond of her, as was my late brother-in-law."

"Shouldn't you be off someplace mourning?"

Shaking his head forlornly, Larry said, "I know I ought to be over at Eva's place, looking after her, but—"

"She's at the office."

"Really? Well, work's a great cure for the blues."

Ben glanced down the track. "You have to go into New York, huh?"

"Yes, exactly. I don't want to at a time like this, but I have an unbreakable lunch date." He shook his head again. "A business thing, with a very successful old college friend. I don't dare break it."

Nodding, Ben asked, "Are you going to be taking over as editor of *Bare?*"

"I haven't actually discussed it with either Dad or my sister, but I imagine I will," he said. "Not that editing that rag is going to put me at the pinnacle of journalistic success."

"Pays better than your current job, though."

He sighed. "It's still extremely difficult to accept the fact that Lloyd's gone." He rubbed at the corner of his eye with a forefinger. "If only I hadn't been running yesterday when it happened."

"You couldn't have prevented it."

"I didn't even get to run my regular route," said Larry. "Because of that stupid molasses spill, I had to make a ridiculous detour. Almost got hopelessly lost twice."

Ben took another look down the track. There was still no sign of the impending train. "That must be an interesting job, though, running things at *Bare.* All those naked women, for instance."

"No, after you've weeded through a ton of pictures, it gets very dull. Tits and ass, tits and ass, tits and ass."

"At least some of the women must stand out, ones with freckles or tattoos."

"I hardly notice any of that anymore."

"On that 'My Best Girl' feature—do guys really send in pictures of their wives, sweethearts, and next of kin?"

"Hundreds of them. You can't imagine, Ben, how many morons there are in the world. We have our fair share around here, but in other parts of the country the percentage has to be much higher."

"When you finally contact the women, to get them to sign a release and all—what are some of them like?"

"Lloyd took care of all the actual paperwork. Just as well, too, since I'd be tempted to tell them they ought to be ashamed of themselves."

"You're going to have to handle all that from now on, though. Did Lloyd keep intelligible files? I hear he hated computers."

Larry chuckled. "Hey, is there one of those amateur models you have a yen for?" he asked. "You're sure curious."

"Actually, Larry," Ben replied in his Bullwinkle voice, "I have a tremendous crush on your grizzly bear mascot."

"Here's the train; want to share a seat?"

"I'd like to, except . . ." Ben patted the empty breast pocket of his suit coat. "Got a couple commercials I really have to concentrate on."

"Sure, I understand. Well, if I don't see you before then, I'll see you at the funeral."

As Ben turned away, he said to himself in his Jiminy Cricket voice, "What did I tell you about lies, Pinoke?"

$\triangledown$

9

AFTER HONKING AT HER twice, the dented red Porsche whipped around H. J.'s car at a narrow, blind stretch of Mott Lane.

"Asshole," she mumbled as the impatient car disappeared over the crest of the hill.

The Porsche was parking in the wide driveway next to the big, white colonial house. Its door came snapping open and a tall, lean man of about forty lunged out of the driver's seat. He was wearing a spotless tan raincoat over a gray business suit and had a tweedy cap on his head.

He ran across the lawn to the oaken front door. He let himself in, slamming the door behind him.

H. J. parked in the drive, as far from the red sports car as she safely could. She sat watching the house for a moment or so. Murmuring, "Over the top," she eased out of the car.

She heard the argument when she was still a hundred feet from the front door.

"Can't you do, for crissake, anything right?" a man was saying loudly.

That must be Earl Wilder, the fellow with the aggressive roadside manner, H. J. thought.

"Don't yell," requested a woman just as loudly. "I've been

very upset by all this, Earl, and your hollering at me doesn't—"

"What did I tell you to do when you phoned me at the goddamn office, Micki?"

"To phone the police, but—"

"So where the fuck are they? It took me twenty-six minutes to drive here from Stamford. Haven't they—"

"I didn't get around to it yet."

By this time H. J. had reached the red brick porch. She stood there, listening.

"Didn't get around to it yet? Shit, Micki."

"If you keep on shouting at me, I—"

"Why didn't you, for Christ sake, get around to it? Our house is broken into while you claim to be out shopping, but you can't even get off your ass to—"

"I *was* shopping, Earl. I can show you the itemized grocery bill from the Village Market if you'd like."

"All you had to do was walk over there and pick up the goddamn phone."

"I'm rattled and upset."

"You've good reason to be, allowing burglars to break into our house and tear it apart. You let them steal us blind and—did they take my new CD player?"

"I didn't *allow* anybody to do anything, dammit. I was out from about half past nine until almost eleven. When I got back, I found the place like this. I sure as hell didn't invite anybody to make this mess."

"So you say."

"Besides, Earl, I don't think they stole much of anything."

"What are you raving about? Of course they stole something. That's what burglars do."

"It's just that I haven't found anything missing so far. I mean, they did pull out all the drawers and toss—"

"Let's call the goddamn cops first. Then we can take an inventory of everything that's missing."

"Okay, go ahead and call them."

"Oh, I'm supposed to make the phone call, huh? One of

your boyfriends probably broke into my house to steal money so he could buy booze and drugs, or maybe extra condoms. But I have to do all the—"

"I'm not fooling around. And if I were, it wouldn't be with a housebreaker. They don't earn enough to interest me."

"What's that supposed to mean? I'm earning almost forty-seven thousand a year at—"

"Call the cops if you're going to."

"I will. After they get here and do their job, Micki, you and I are going to have a talk."

Reaching out, H. J. pushed the door bell.

"Now what the hell is that?" shouted Wilder.

"Somebody at the door."

"Well, answer it and get rid of them. Probably another one of your boyfriends. He'll be surprised to find me at home."

A moment later the door was opened a few inches. A pretty, dark-haired woman of about H. J.'s age looked out at her. "Yes?"

H. J. smiled innocently. "Good morning. I'm with the Wilton Bible Society and—"

"This, honestly, isn't a really good time to call."

"Who the hell is it?" The door was yanked open wider and Earl Wilder glared out.

Smiling again, H. J. said, "Good morning, sir. I'm glad to find both of you at home. I'm with the Wilton Bible Society and we're—"

"Go away." Pivoting on his heel, he went striding toward a phone. He was still wearing his raincoat.

"You'd better go," Micki advised her.

Leaning close, H. J. asked, "Did Lloyd Dobkin leave any of his files with you?"

"What?"

"Did Lloyd—"

"I'm afraid I don't know anyone by that name."

Wilder was yelling into the receiver, "How do you expect me to have the damn number for the police? You're supposed to know it, operator."

"I'd hate," said H. J. softly, "to have to discuss all this with your husband."

After glancing over her shoulder, the dark-haired woman stepped out onto the porch and shut the door. "Listen, is that what this break-in is all about? Does someone think Lloyd left some of his stuff here?"

"I think so, yes. Did he?"

She shook her head. "Good lord, no. He knew better than that," she answered in a whisper. "My husband just about stages a white-glove inspection when he gets home from work every night. You couldn't hide a dead gnat in this house without Earl's finding the damn thing."

"Can you think of anywhere else Lloyd might have left—"

"Who are you anyway?"

"H. J. Mavity. My husband and I are trying—"

"Oh, I recognize you now. I saw your picture in the paper. You were with him when he got killed."

"I was. We think maybe he hid something important with one of his friends."

"Jesus, does somebody think I've got it?"

"You must be on their list."

"But, like I told you, he never would've considered stashing a damn thing here."

"Did he talk to you about a big, new story he was in the middle of?"

Micki shook her head. "Ours wasn't a relationship that involved much confiding—on either side," she said. "This stuff they're searching for—it's Lloyd's notes on something?"

"Probably."

"Would they be worth a lot, do you think?"

"Well, somebody sure thinks they are."

"I don't like the idea that—"

"They're coming right over," announced Wilder after jerking the door open wide. "Get on inside. She can't talk to you anymore, ma'am."

"I was just leaving," H. J. informed him pleasantly. "God bless you both."

$\triangledown$

10

Ben had a train seat to himself. He was holding on
tightly to his copy of *The New York Times*, struggling to
keep awake. You heard a lot about the stress of commuting,
but this particular ride was having a very soothing effect.

His eyelids yearned to snap shut, his body was seriously
considering slumping. He felt snores stockpiling in his nose.

Having H. J. back in his life might seriously disrupt his
sleep patterns.

Sitting up straighter, shaking his head several times, he
took a few deep breaths, mouth open.

That was better.

He forced himself to concentrate on Vincent Canby's re-
view of a new Gerard Depardieu farce that was apparently
both delightful and astonishingly diverting.

"I used to be diverting," he said to himself in his Charles
Boyer voice.

Then his head commenced drifting over toward the window beside him. Abruptly he made the transition from being
awake to being asleep.

He was in Boston with a hot yellow sun blazing directly
above. He was wearing the shorts he'd borrowed from the
man on the station platform.

The idea was that he had to win the Boston Marathon—win, not merely come in second or third—or something astonishingly terrible was going to happen to H. J.

Ben was jogging along with at least a thousand other runners, but he was having a hell of a time making any progress. That was mainly because the street was filled, knee high, with dark, sticky molasses.

"You can't run through molasses," he complained to Sankowitz, who was now slogging along beside him.

"Just ignore it," advised the cartoonist.

Thunk!

Ben's head banged the window and he awakened.

He cleared his throat, trying to give the impression, in case anyone had noticed, that he hadn't actually fallen asleep at all.

Very carefully, he shut his *Times*, folded it, and placed it on the empty seat beside him.

Resting both hands on his knees, he took a few more slow, careful breaths.

Suddenly he sat up and said aloud, "Molasses."

A gray-haired man across the aisle, banker or stockbroker almost certainly, frowned briefly at him.

"It's my mantra," he explained, grinning in a way he hoped would make him seem harmless.

There'd been molasses spilled all over Post Road in Brimstone yesterday. H. J. had told him about it, and there'd been a story in the paper. The stuff had filled the street at about 12:40 P.M. or so.

But Larry Dahlman had claimed to be running. Straight up Rivergate Road, across Post Road and beyond before turning back for the office again. Did it every day. And he'd told H. J., just after the killing, that he'd done the exact same thing yesterday.

But he couldn't have run up that way and across Post Road, because that intersection would've been closed to both cars and foot traffic by the time he got there.

This morning, just now on the platform, Larry had given

him an amended story. He was claiming today that he'd run an alternate route. That was because he'd found out about the spill between the time he'd talked to H. J. and the time he talked to Ben.

A small point probably.

But why had he lied about it? And which version of his run had he given to the police? Well, maybe neither. They probably hadn't questioned him in any detail.

It was possible, though, that he hadn't been running during the time of the killing.

Okay, but it could be that he was shacked up with somebody's wife and didn't want to mention it. Or maybe he was simply off having a pizza and a couple of brews and thought that would spoil his jock image with H. J.

So why's he rushing into the Apple today?

His brother-in-law has just been killed, his sister is taking over the running of the Dahlman publications. His place was in Brimstone.

But he obviously had an important meeting with somebody in New York City.

Ben figured he ought to be able to find out who the meeting was with. Larry was on the same train, and he simply had to follow him.

He would have about a half hour after getting into the city before the lunch at the Hotel Dunkirk started. He'd use the time to tail Larry Dahlman.

He picked up the newspaper again. He felt wide awake.

Larry didn't go far.

From Grand Central he led Ben along Forty-sixth Street over to Third Avenue. Looming up in midblock was a new glass and metal building.

"Well, blow me down," exclaimed Ben in his Popeye voice when he realized where his quarry must be heading.

It was the Timberlake Building.

Striding rapidly, Larry pushed through the revolving doors.

Ben had kept a quarter block behind him. As he approached the doors himself, he slowed to take a look up at the glistening building. Even on an overcast day, it seemed to glow.

Suppose Sue Ellen Timberlake were alive somewhere? She'd own all this.

Or a goodly part of it anyway. At least the first twenty or so floors.

Just as he reached the doors, they spun and disgorged someone.

"Exactly the person I most want to see. Were you coming to visit me, Benjy?"

Laura Timberlake Barks was about ten pounds heavier than when last he'd encountered her, her hair a deeper shade of brown. She was tanned, wearing an obviously expensive suit and no makeup or jewelry.

"Oh, are you *that* Timberlake?" He tried to look beyond her and into the building lobby. "Actually, Laura, I was merely passing by."

"You obviously don't love me."

"Oh, so?"

"You haven't hugged me or kissed me."

"Does doing an occasional radio spot for Sudz give me hugging privileges?"

"We're old pals, aren't we? Many's the time you've saved my sanity during a commercial recording session."

Nodding, he asked, "You heading for the awards lunch?"

"Yes." She took hold of his arm. "Mostly because I was informed you were a shoo-in for a Pete award for those wonderful Sudz spots you did for us."

"A Paul award."

"Whatever. Some sort of prestigious dornick."

"Is your affable brother in town?"

She pointed her free thumb in the direction of the Timberlake Building. "Don T.'s up in his playpen," she answered. "Much too busy, he claims, for the lunch."

"A pity."

"Yes, isn't it? Probably many of your acting and advertising cronies haven't as yet seen the biggest schmuck in this part of the world." She dragged him over to the curb. "I'll give you a lift to the hotel, Benjy."

"Fine. Have I, by the way, ever mentioned that, because of eccentric christening notions of my mother's, my complete and total first name is Ben. So there's no need to call me any diminutives of Benjamin."

"Would you be interested in, oh, one hundred thousand dollars?"

"Just for allowing you to continue calling me Benjy?"

A long, gray limousine pulled quietly up to the curb. A slim Hispanic young man in a flawless white suit rushed from the driver's seat and came around to bow to Laura. Then he opened the rear door for her.

"Gracias, Miguelito." Smiling, she slid into the shadowy interior of the limo.

Ducking, Ben followed. "About the hundred thousand—is it a bribe?"

"You may not have heard yet," she told him as the driver eased the limo back into traffic, "but we're starting to test-market a new product. Sudz, Jr."

"Laundry soap for kids?"

"Exactly, Ben. Our agency on this account—Nolan and Anmar here in town—has come up with a cute little kid to be a sort of mascot and spokesperson. Baby Bubbles."

"Very cute."

"You'd be absolutely perfect to do the voice of the little putz." She took hold of his arm again. "It must have been fate that brought us together just now."

"Not quite," he said.

11

As H. J. STARTED ACROSS the parking lot, the front door of Dahlman's dark limo swung silently open.

A large, wide-shouldered blond man in a tight-fitting dark suit stepped out into the gray afternoon. Smiling shyly, he nodded in her direction. "Ms. Mavity, is it?" he asked in a voice faintly tinted with a Scandinavian accent.

She stopped. "Yes."

"I'm Bjornsen."

"Yes, so I've heard."

The big chauffeur inclined his head toward the rear door of the limousine. "If you'd mind standing there for a moment, Ms. Mavity?"

"What's this for—a Civil Defense test?"

"Mr. Dahlman would like a word."

She rested her portfolio against her leg and frowned at the tinted side window. "He's in there?"

The window slid silently halfway open. A very old hand, leathery, etched with intricate wrinkles, blotched with age spots, appeared and clutched the top of the rolled-down glass. There was a large gold ring on the ring finger and a soiled plastic bandage on the knuckle of the forefinger.

"Helen Joanne," said a dry, whispery voice from within. "We've never met."

All she could see through the opening was shadows. "That's true, Mr. Dahlman."

"You're quite pretty."

"Thank you."

Bjornsen had stationed himself near the hood. He was standing there, arms folded, gazing out toward the river.

The unseen Dahlman said, "Perhaps you can tell me something, young lady."

"Perhaps, sure."

"You were with my unfortunate son-in-law when he passed on."

She nodded.

"Did he . . . confide anything in you?"

"Only what I told the police."

"Sometimes we don't tell the police everything." The bandaged forefinger began tapping, very slowly, on the edge of the dark window glass.

"This wasn't one of those times."

"Lloyd didn't mention my daughter?"

"Nope."

"Or any other member of my family?"

"Nary a one, no."

"He didn't tell you where you might . . . find something?"

"He didn't."

"Thank you, my dear." The hand retreated into the darkness, the window shut.

"Well, nice meeting you," she told the window.

The driver was still watching the nearby river.

Picking up her portfolio, H. J. continued on into the Dahlman Building.

Eva, who was wearing black, unlocked the door to her late husband's office and said, "You see, dear? It's terrible."

From the threshold H. J. surveyed the editor's room. It had been recently ransacked and hundreds of color photos and slides of naked young women were strewn on the floor. "Any notion who did it?" she asked the widow.

"Could have been anyone." She shut the door, locked it again, and beckoned H. J. to follow her back to her own office. "*Bare* has a rather cheesy readership, and God knows which of our demented fans took advantage of the situation to break in and swipe nude photos."

"But did they actually steal any photographs? Seems like there are a ton of them on the floor in there."

"Lloyd must have had *two* tons of them stashed in there. He never threw a damn thing out." Eva returned to her desk, seating herself in the large black leather chair. "I used to tell him all that clutter was an eyesore, but he . . ." She trailed off, began sobbing. She yanked a tissue from a japanned box atop her wide metal desk.

H. J. sat in a chair facing her. "You have an alarm system. Why didn't it go off when they broke in?"

"There was such confusion here yesterday, with police coming and going, and reporters. Anybody could have slipped into the building unnoticed."

"It seems unlikely that anyone would trash his office while the cops were still on the premises. They must have waited until last night."

"Well, that's possible, dear. I don't know whether anyone remembered, in all the confusion and stress, to set the alarm system when we finally left yesterday." She blew her nose.

"Do you have any idea who killed Lloyd?"

Eva plucked a fresh tissue to blow her nose again. "I'm sure you were aware that he wasn't especially loyal to me. We were fond of each other, you understand, but Lloyd did tomcat around a good deal."

"What are you suggesting—a jealous husband or an angry lover?"

"Yes, that's certainly possible, considering all the women he's fooled around with. Someone may have decided to . . . well, to punish him."

"You think that's who searched his office?"

Eva learned forward. "You say *searched* rather than robbed, dear. Do you have reason to believe that Lloyd had some specific thing of value hidden in there?"

"It just doesn't appear that much, if anything, was stolen. But it sure looks like somebody was hunting for something," she answered, opening her portfolio. "Here's the *Love's Claimant* rough that Lloyd approved."

Eva took the drawing but didn't look at it. "As Lloyd lay dying, did he say anything to you?"

"Nothing much. Certainly there were no dying messages."

"Not a word to indicate that he might have, oh, stumbled onto something lucrative?"

"Nope, nothing like that." H. J. shook her head. "What makes you ask?"

"You've started me thinking, and it occurs to me that lately, the past few weeks, Lloyd had been acting somewhat smug," the widow confided. "Well, he could be annoyingly smug a good deal of the time, but this was somewhat different. Maybe finally he really was on the brink of striking it rich."

"He didn't confide anything like that to me."

"As his widow, after all, I stand to benefit from anything like that."

"That's certainly true. But if Lloyd did have a lucrative secret, it died with him," she lied. "What about the cover?"

"The cover? Oh, yes, that is why I asked you here, isn't it?" Eva, brow wrinkling, studied the rough she was holding. "We need more cleavage, dear."

"So Lloyd mentioned."

"Also, I'm having the logo redesigned and made somewhat larger. You'll have to leave another half inch here and here to fit it in."

"That's no problem, Eva."

"All right, go paint us the cover then. Lloyd trusted you and so do I." She returned the cover sketch.

Dropping it in her portfolio, H. J. stood. "I'll have the finished art for you in a week or so."

"Fine, and keep in mind that even though dear Lloyd is gone, there'll still be a lot more assignments here for you."

"I won't be taking on any further assignments after this one, but thanks."

"So you're going back to Ben and giving up your career?"

"Nope, I'm going back to Ben and taking my career in some new directions." She crossed to the door.

"You escaped once, dear." Eva shook her head, sighing. "It seems a real shame to go back."

$\triangledown$

12

H.J. HADN'T INTENDED to break any further promises.

After her meeting with Eva, she'd come straight home to Ben's. She intended to finish cleaning up in the wake of the housebreakers.

This was also her night to fix dinner, and she'd have to start thinking about that problem soon.

A few minutes short of four the phone rang.

"Mavity-Spanner residence."

"Oh, dearie me, I must have the wrong number," said Ben in his little old lady voice. "What I wanted, child, was the Spanner-Mavity residence."

"Where are you?"

In his own voice he replied, "Still in New York, which is why I'm—"

"Did you win?"

"The award, you mean? Matter of fact, yes."

"Congratulations. It's nice when your peers—"

"Listen, H. J., I'm up at the Nolan and Anmar ad agency. They want me for a voice in a new Sudz campaign and I have to sit in on a meeting. Starts at four and should run at least an hour. So don't look for me until after six."

"Speaking of Timberlake products, was she at the festivities?"

"Yep."

"Well?"

"And right now she's sitting one office over from here."

"So you can't talk?"

"Not with ease, no."

"Did you find out anything?"

"Some."

"Well, is she involved? Is the family aware that Lloyd—"

"I'm not sure. I'll—yes, dear, it's a cute baby character I'm doing. Should be great fun."

"Intruders?"

"Exactly. See you around sundown. And stay close to hearth and home, huh?"

"But of course. I already promised that I would, didn't I?"

After hanging up, H. J. resumed gathering books off the floor.

Why had Laura Timberlake Barks offered Ben a job?

Well, maybe she hadn't. It could be the agency thought of hiring Ben entirely on its own and this was just a coincidence.

But it had to be deliberate, didn't it? They must want to keep an eye on him, pump him subtly, too.

But how did they know that Ben had any knowledge of Lloyd's search for the Timberlake heiress?

The newspapers had mentioned that H. J. was there when Lloyd got killed. And quite a few people knew she and Ben were together once again.

Frowning, she wandered into the kitchen.

"Damn it, I don't want anything to happen to him."

She opened the refrigerator, began scanning its contents in search of an inspiration for tonight's meal.

"Maybe I can stir fry something."

There was a considerable quantity of snow peas in one of the crisper drawers.

And in the meat bin, a small amount of steak.

"I really should be working on the case." She walked over and sat at the kitchen table, resting an elbow on it. "The sooner all this gets cleared up, the sooner Ben and I are out of danger."

She popped to her feet.

The thing to do was find Lloyd's files. As soon as possible.

H. J. decided to visit Alicia Bertillion over in Redding Ridge. She'd certainly be able to take care of that before Ben got back from the city.

Grabbing her tan jacket from the hall closet, she hurried out of the house.

She didn't become fully aware of the car following her until she'd been driving nearly five minutes. Glancing into the rearview mirror, she noticed it.

It looked like a Fiero, several years old and a dusty black. She couldn't make out the driver because the windshield was deeply tinted.

H. J. realized that the black car had been with her since she left home, trailing her, keeping about a hundred yards from her tail.

"Easy now," she advised herself, "let's not get too paranoid."

It might be the Fiero just happened to be going in the same direction she was.

When the next lane intersected, H. J. whipped her car onto it and speeded up.

A moment later the black car appeared behind her again.

She was passing by large houses set back on two acres and more. Trees, hedges, and an occasional stone fence lined the narrow roadway.

At the next intersection she swung abruptly to the left, gunned her car uphill, and then turned right on the first new road she came to.

The Fiero kept with her.

"This isn't television," she reminded herself. "Nobody's

likely to drive by and let loose with an automatic weapon."

Even so, she wished the damn car weren't behind her.

Up ahead at the side of the road, two girls of about eight or nine had set up a juice stand.

One of them was holding a hand-lettered sign up above her head—"Cool Drinks! 25¢!"

H. J. slowed the car, pulled off the road, and stopped. Dropping her keys into her shoulder bag, she said, "Might as well meet the son of a bitch in front of witnesses."

She slid free of her car, and walked over to the makeshift stand. "You didn't pick a very good day to go into this particular business," she said to the girls. "What flavors?"

"All we have is grape juice," said the girl who wasn't holding the sign. She patted the side of the plastic bucket sitting atop the stand. Her hair was braided and almost the same shade as H. J.'s.

"Grape, huh?"

The dusty Fiero appeared on the road. It didn't stop, but drove slowly on by.

The side windows were tinted, too, and H. J. couldn't see the driver at all.

The car continued on, crested the hill, and was gone.

"I've decided I'm not thirsty." Smiling, she gave each of the girls a quarter. "But, thanks, anyway."

Hurrying back to her car, she started it and turned quickly around. She drove back in the direction she'd come.

She drove onto a small winding lane, then down another rustic road. After about ten minutes of zigzagging over hill and dale, she was certain she'd ditched her tail.

She resumed her journey to Alicia Bertillion's, using an alternate route.

The illustrator lived in a converted barn in a hilly stretch of town. The big russet house sat in a clearing amidst several acres of woodland. Alicia Bertillion had no immediate neighbors.

H. J. parked on the white gravel of the driveway. A light

rain was starting up, and a few preliminary raindrops hit her as she left the car and ran across a stretch of yellowed lawn.

She climbed the front steps of the onetime barn. Then she noticed that the bright red door was open several inches.

Moving closer to the opening, she called out, "Hello? Anybody home?"

There was no reply.

Gingerly, H. J. reached out and pushed the door all the way open.

She entered the big, beam-ceilinged living room.

She sneezed twice.

The room had been ransacked, and over in front of the deep red brick fireplace was sprawled the body of a gray-haired woman.

▽

13

ALICIA BERTILLION WASN'T DEAD.

She'd been knocked out, and as H. J. approached her, she moaned and began to regain consciousness.

Kneeling beside her, H. J. took hold of her hand. "Take it easy," she said. "I'll phone the paramedics and they'll—"

"No, don't phone anybody." The gray-haired woman struggled to sit up.

"You've got a lump on your head and—"

"I also have a career doing kids' books." With help from H. J., she achieved a sitting position. "I have an idea what this is probably about. That sort of publicity I don't need."

"You mean it has to do with Lloyd Dobkin?"

Alicia eyed her. "Who are you, by the way?"

"H. J. Mavity. I'm an artist, too."

"I don't know your work."

"That puts you in the majority. I do a lot of paperback covers, and Lloyd was a friend of mine," she explained. "But not the sort of friend he was to you."

"Oh, that's right. You're the one who was with him," she said as H. J. helped her over to a soft armchair. "It really was murder and not just an accident?"

"Yes, there's no doubt of that." Skirting a spill of a half-dozen copies of *Tammy the Turtle,* she sat on the arm of a tan leather sofa. "Now, what happened here?"

"I did something stupid."

"Which was?"

"I walked in on the man."

"You saw him?"

Alicia smiled thinly. "More to the point, H. J., he saw me," she answered. "Then he conked me with a blackjack. First time I've ever seen one in real life."

"Did your recognize him?"

Touching the place where she'd been hit and then wincing, Alicia said, "He was wearing a ski mask. A big man, in a dark windbreaker and slacks."

"People you're familiar with, even if masked, you ought to be able to recognize by body movements, bone structure, and such," H. J. said. "Was this guy anybody you knew?"

"It's my impression he wasn't someone I was familiar with."

"Did the guy say anything?"

"Not a word," she answered. "I heard some noise in here, and, daredevil that I am, I charged right in to see what was the matter. He grabbed me and hit me a good one."

"You sure you're okay? A blow on the head can—"

"I'll be fine, really." She leaned back, watching H. J. for a few silent seconds. "Why exactly did you come here?"

"To ask you if Lloyd had left any of his files with you."

"So I was right. This hoodlum was hunting for something he thought Lloyd may have given me to keep for him."

"Were you keeping anything?"

"No, I wasn't." She shook her head, which caused her to grimace with pain.

"But you knew he had something valuable to hide?"

"He'd been talking about a discovery that was going to make him rich."

"Did he give you any details?"

"Very few," said Alicia. "It had something to do with a crime in the past, but he didn't tell me which one. Lloyd, you know, used to do a lot of crime writing."

"Do you have any idea where he did put his notes and all?"

"Yes, I think I do," she said. "About a week ago, after he started worrying that someone was trying to do him harm, he told me he'd stuck his important notes on this business in a small strongbox and hidden it."

"Did he say where?"

"All he told me was that he'd stashed the box at St. Swithin's. But that isn't the name of any church around here."

"St. Swithin's, huh?" said H. J., grinning slowly. "I know where it is."

"It's actually a church?"

"Lloyd's nickname for one."

"If you're planning to go there and hunt for that box," warned the illustrator, "you could get hurt." She touched again at the lump on her head.

"I won't go until after dark," she said. "And I'll take my husband along for protection."

Ben didn't get home until after eight-thirty that evening. The meeting at the advertising agency had dragged on until almost six o'clock. And then, because he was definitely going to be doing the Baby Bubbles voice for Sudz, Jr., both Nolan and Anmar had insisted on buying him a drink at their favorite spot of the moment, a dreary Irish pub on East Forty-ninth.

He had hoped to get a chance for more verbal fencing with Laura Timberlake Barks, but she'd slipped away before the meeting was over. She had thrown him a kiss, but that didn't add any information to his store.

The earliest train that he was able to catch out of the city was the 7:06.

The rain was falling enthusiastically again as he drove onto his property. Through the downpour he noticed that there wasn't a single light on in the house. "Damn it, where's she gotten to?"

Stowing the car in the otherwise empty garage, Ben hurried into the dark house.

"Honey, I'm home," he called out in his Dagwood Bumstead voice.

As he'd anticipated, there was no answer.

He turned on several lights and looked around the living room.

The answering machine indicated there were two messages waiting. Sitting on the sofa in a ready-to-jump position, he hit the play button.

"It's Joe. I'm curious about what foolhardy actions you folks have undertaken since last we met. Call me."

"Yeah, okay. Next."

"Mr. or Mrs. Spanner. This is Bob Lichty of Weiner and Weiner Investments in Westport. Call me if you want to double your—"

"You're wasting my time, asshole." He jabbed the stop button and jumped to his feet.

No note from H. J. on the dining-room table.

Nothing on the kitchen table either.

But stuck to the front of the refrigerator with the Minnie Mouse magnet was a scribbled note: "Ben, I hope you won't explode. But I waited until nearly eight o'clock and then got the fidgets. Soon as you get home meet me at the Brimstone Denominational Church. I'll probably be poking around in the old graveyard. Love, your ex."

"The graveyard?" Folding up the note, he slipped it into his coat pocket.

Not bothering to change clothes, he ran back to the garage. If he was going to be prowling around in a cemetery, he ought to be wearing something other than one of his Manhattan suits. But Ben felt he couldn't spare the time.

▽

14

"Damn," observed H. J. as she parked under a stand of oak trees across the street from the venerable old church she'd used as the model for St. Swithin's on the cover of *Love's Claimant*, "I wasn't expecting this."

On the wide field between the Gothic-style church and the nineteenth-century graveyard three large candy-striped tents had been pitched. Several floodlights were set up, and in their glare she saw a dozen or more people moving in and out of the tents. Those going in were toting small appliances, bundles of clothes, boxes of books.

On a post driven into the grass was a handsomely lettered sign announcing a "Gala Rummage Sale" coming up this Thursday and Friday.

All these unanticipated people must be helping the Brimstone Denominational Church get ready for the event.

H. J. sat there for a moment, watching the illuminated activity across the way. The night rain tap-danced on the roof of her car.

"Well, Ben's not the only actor in the family," she said, taking a small flashlight from the glove compartment and stowing it in her shoulder bag.

Outside in the rain, H. J. hurried around to the trunk.
She had a carton of discarded clothes in there that she'd been
meaning to drop off at the Goodwill.

Gathering up the box and slamming the trunk shut with
her elbow, she crossed the street and walked right on into
the nearest tent.

Near the entrance, a thin blond woman in jeans and a
Harvard sweatshirt was pricing items on a table cluttered
with odds and ends. She smiled at H. J.

Smiling sweetly back, H. J. said, "Sorry I'm late. I'm Mrs.
Spanner and we're new to the church, but Mrs.—gosh, I
can't remember her name. Plump woman, gray hair?"

"That'd be Mrs. Brinkerhoff. She's up in tent three, the
one right next to the old graveyard."

"That's her, yes," said H. J., nodding. "She told me to drop
this stuff here, and then maybe I could help out."

"We can always use more help. I'm Eleanor Reisberson."

"Nice to meet you. Shall I just leave this box here someplace and then go report to Mrs. Brinkerhoff?"

"That's clothes, so you better turn it over to Mrs. Tooker."

H. J. glanced around at the other people in the tent. "Gee,
I forget which one she is."

"She's wearing those green overalls."

"Oh, yes, I see her. I'll do that."

After abandoning the carton to Mrs. Tooker, H. J. went
back out into the rainswept night.

She trudged up through the wet field in the direction of
the third tent.

A chubby man in a yellow raincoat came downhill toward
her, lugging a metal tub filled with mismatched dishware.
"Really coming down tonight, isn't it?"

"That it is," she agreed.

She walked right on by the last tent and Mrs. Brinkerhoff.
The illumination from the floodlights, she noted, didn't spill
over into most of the old burial ground.

Sloshing through mud and puddles and wishing she'd had
the sense to wear boots, H. J. made her way to the ancient

wrought-iron gates in the stone wall that surrounded the graveyard.

She didn't think Lloyd would have hidden anything in the church itself or in the rectory. But he had been fond of roaming in this old cemetery, and it seemed a likely place for him to have stashed his strongbox.

Pushing the iron gates slowly and carefully open, she slipped inside.

It took her nearly fifteen minutes to spot a small patch of ground that showed evidence of recent digging. By that time the rain had ceased.

Since no one had been buried here after the turn of the century, this sign of recent activity suggested to her that this was where Lloyd had hidden his files.

Resting her flashlight on a flat marble slab dedicated to the memory of Daniel Guild 1810–1884, she fished out the trowel she'd brought along in her bag.

Less than six inches below the ground she struck something metallic. After five minutes of diligent digging and scooping, she unearthed a black metal box. It looked just large enough to accommodate several file folders.

The muddy box was locked, but the screwdriver she'd also brought along was sufficient to pry open the lid and snap the small lock.

H. J. opened the box and pointed her light at the contents. "Bingo," she said, pleased.

Inside rested a thick manila folder with "Timberlake Matter" lettered across the cover in Lloyd's familiar scrawl.

Unmindful of the dampness, H. J. perched on the tombstone of Joshua Bascom 1821–1889 and lifted the cover of the folder.

Inside she found five color photographs of an attractive, naked young woman, a blond in her middle twenties. There were three front views and two rear; the picture that Lloyd had entrusted to her was a blowup of part of one of the rearviews. This was definitely the woman with the butterfly birthmark.

On the back of each picture was stamped "Mark Juster—
Photographer, Box 226, Willmur, Mass. 02171."

Unfortunately the name of the model wasn't there.

The folder also contained Lloyd's old notes on the
Timberlake kidnapping, plus photocopies of the baby's hospital records, including a footprint.

H. J. skimmed through everything in the folder, but didn't
find anything that mentioned the blond model's name.

"Even so, this is a great leap forward." She shoved everything back inside the folder, stuffed it into the box, and shut
the lid. Clicking off her flash, she tucked the box up under
her arm.

She started back down toward her car, smiling with satisfaction. "If Ben shows up about now, he's really going to be
pleased with me."

She was opposite the stand of dark oaks, still several yards
from her car, when she became aware of a familiar scent
behind her.

H. J. started to turn, but something smacked her hard
across the back of the neck.

She staggered, legs going wobbly.

She heard the metal box smack the ground. Then, hit
again from behind, she passed out.

Ben was about two miles from the old church when he began
to feel uneasy. He'd been hearing sirens for the past few
minutes, and now an ambulance, lights flashing, came
racing up the road behind him.

He swung over to the roadside, letting it go wailing by.

"Relax, my boy," he advised himself in his Sigmund Freud
voice, "you're letting your imagination run away with you."

There were all sorts of reasons for an ambulance to be
heading for this part of town. Most likely it was a fire, which
would explain the other sirens. The odds were that none of
this had anything to do with H. J.

"She should have waited for me, though."

When he reached the Brimstone Denominational

Church, he saw two police cars, a paramedic van, and the ambulance all parked in the middle of the slick street.

Two white-coated attendants loaded a stretcher into the ambulance and then drove off.

The field on Ben's right had three big tents pitched on it for some reason, and about twenty people were standing in front of them staring across the street.

He noticed H. J.'s car then. It was circled by the police cars and the van, and its driver-side door was open wide.

A uniformed cop was shining his torch into the front seat.

"Jesus!" He left his car where it was, motor still running, and jumped free to hurry across the wet night road.

Another cop stepped in front of him when he got close. "There's been an accident, sir. You'll have to move back out of the way, please."

"My wife. That's her car. Where is she?"

The other officer moved back from the driver's seat and turned around. "You're Ben Spanner, aren't you?"

"Right, Officer Thompson. That's my wife's car. What happened?"

"Let him come on over, Andy," said Thompson, a heavyset blond man.

"Is she in there?"

"No, she was found on the sidewalk beside her car."

"Found? Is she dead?"

The officer shook his head. "No, sir, Mr. Spanner. But someone hit her on the head and knocked her cold."

Ben swallowed, then pointed in the direction the ambulance had gone. "That was her in the ambulance?"

"Yeah, they're taking her to the emergency wing at Brimstone General."

"Do you know what happened?"

A lean, bearded man in a clerical suit came over to them. "I'm Father Hellinger," he said. "I found the young woman. All we know is that she was hit over the head and fell there beside the car."

"Is it a fracture, a concussion?"

"There was some bleeding," the priest said, "but I can't guess at the exact nature of the injury."

Ben glanced around. "Her things?"

"Someone had gone through her shoulder bag. We gathered up the contents, put them back in the bag, and sent that along with her."

"I've got to get over there right away."

Father Hellinger caught his arm. "Try to keep calm, Mr. Spanner," he advised. "Drive carefully."

"Yes, sure, I will. Thanks."

"We'll pray for her," promised the priest as Ben ran back to his car.

$\triangledown$

15

AFTER TWO TRIES BEN got one of the nurses behind the long, white emergency counter to notice him. "It's about my wife," he began. "She was just brought in and—"

"The maternity ward is on the next level up, sir."

"No doubt it is. But she was hit on the head, and I'm trying to find out how serious the—"

"Oh, that would be Ms. Mavity, wouldn't it?" The thin, dark-haired nurse picked up a metal clipboard from the counter.

"That's her, yeah. How serious is—"

"And you're Mr. Mavity?"

"Actually I'm Ben Spanner. Now, what sort of—"

"What is your relationship to the patient?"

"She's my wife. That is, she used to be my wife."

"Is this injury the result of some domestic squabble?"

"No, from her poking around an old cemetery, I think. The point is, what exactly—"

"How is the bill going to be handled, sir?"

Ben took a slow, careful breath. He rested both palms on the counter and looked directly across at the thin nurse. "First tell me how seriously she's been hurt," he requested. "After that we'll talk about the bill."

"Ms. Mavity is in an emergency room with Dr. Mc-Clennan now, sir," she answered. "Is she covered by your medical insurance or—"

"Can I go in and see her?"

"Not yet, sir. Or does Ms. Mavity carry her own—oh, this is Dr. McClennan."

A medium-sized black intern had appeared behind the counter and taken the clipboard from her. "Yes?" he said, glancing across at Ben.

"H. J. Mavity is my wife. My ex-wife. How is she?"

The doctor made a few notations on the chart. "There was a moderate laceration of the scalp at the rear of the skull, and that required six stitches," he replied. "Also a modest hematoma. She was hit hard enough to put her into a semicoma-tose state, though there's no fracture and probably not even a concussion. But, with a head injury such as hers, she ought to spend the night here so that we can keep an eye on her."

"But far as you can tell, she's okay?"

"Yes, though I do want to run a few more tests."

"Can I see her now?"

"Yes, but only for a few minutes." Coming out from be-hind the counter, he led Ben down a green corridor.

Behind the curtains of one of the emergency rooms they passed an elderly man was complaining, "How the hell can I take a piss if I'm not supposed to get off this goddamn bed?"

H. J., wearing a light blue hospital gown, was in the next room. She was sitting up on the emergency table, legs crossed, scowling. She looked very pale, and the back of her head was bandaged. "Ben," she said in a thin voice. "Things have gone somewhat awry."

Putting his arms carefully around her, he kissed her on the cheek. "You okay?"

"About as well as can be expected," she said, hugging him. "This shade of blue, by the way, doesn't suit me at all and there's too much ventilation."

"Listen, they think you should spend the night in a room here. That way—"

"Hooey. I'm fine," she insisted. "Well, not fine, but passable. Gather my clothes and—"

"Ms. Mavity," put in the doctor, "it really isn't wise."

"Can you force me to stay?"

"No, yet I really—"

"Ben, help me get my clothes."

"Whoa now." He stepped back from her. "You've had a head injury, and you're not going to risk some serious side effects by leaving the hospital too soon."

"We don't have time for me to loll around in here overnight."

"You're more important, Helen Joanne, than—"

"Doctor, may I speak to him alone, please?"

"Yes, certainly." Dr. McClennan withdrew.

Sitting on the cot beside her, Ben put an arm around her waist. "Who hit you?"

"We'll get to that in a minute," she told him. "First, I found Lloyd's file. With the pictures of the Timberlake heiress and all."

"But you don't have the stuff now?"

"I was hijacked," she admitted forlornly. "There was no manila folder among my effects when I woke up here. I asked. Now, make a note of this name and address before I forget it. Mark Juster, Box 226, Willmur, Mass. I don't remember the zip. Did you write that down on something, Ben?"

"I'm a quick study. I'll remember."

"Repeat it then."

"Mark Juster, Box 226, Willmur, Mass. Who is he?"

"He's the gonzo who took the pictures of the butterfly woman."

"Was her name in the notes?"

"No, Lloyd may have hidden that someplace else." She took hold of his hand. "You've got to phone Juster, warn him to look after the woman."

Ben asked, "Do you know who hit you and swiped the file?"

She said, "Larry."

"Larry Dahlman?"

"That Larry, yes. I didn't actually see the bastard, but I smelled him," she said. "You've got to get over to his place and retrieve that file. It may be too late, but—"

"Yeah, I'm anxious to have a chat with him. In fact, most anybody who's bopped you on the coco is—"

"Excuse me." Dr. McClennan had returned. "We really have to take care of getting you into a room, Ms. Mavity. There are a few more tests that ought to be done."

"All right," H. J. conceded. "I guess I *had* better spend the night. I really do feel sort of wretched."

Ben said, "Phone me in the morning, and I'll come spring you."

"Be careful if you have to do any housebreaking," she told him. "Don't lose your temper if you run into Larry. The file has 'Timberlake Matter' written on the cover. And warn Juster."

"I'll do all that and more." After kissing her again, he left the small white room.

The doctor followed him into the corridor. "I'm a bit concerned, Mr. Spanner," he confided. "She seems to be babbling in an irrational way."

"To the outside world she frequently gives that impression," explained Ben. "Actually, trust me, everything she's been saying makes perfect sense."

"Obviously you understand her better than I do."

"A little better," he admitted.

Ben reached Larry Dahlman's ranch-style house in the nearby town of Weston at a few minutes shy of eleven. There was light showing at several of the windows, and in the open garage he saw Larry's Mercedes.

Dozens of trees dotted the acre and a half of ground, and a low stone fence separated the property from the nearest neighbor. Downhill somewhere a dog tried a few mournful howls and then fell silent.

Using the brass gargoyle knocker, Ben gave the front door several resounding whaps.

Nothing happened.

He knocked on the door with his fist.

Off in the night the dog howled again.

Larry still didn't show up to answer the door.

Reaching out, Ben tried the handle. The door was locked.

Next he undertook a slow circuit of the house. The drapes were drawn tight on the living-rooms, so he wasn't able to get a look inside.

At the rear of the place, he discovered that a panel of glass had been smashed out of the laundry-room door. Using his handkerchief, he turned the knob.

The door swung open inward.

After counting slowly to ten, listening as he stood there, he entered the house.

Moving cautiously, he checked out each room. Larry wasn't there, though the powerful smell of his aftershave was everywhere.

In the living room, a chair was lying with its legs in the air, a broken lamp lay beside it. In front of the fireplace he found several fresh spots of blood on the tan carpeting.

Next to the sofa, which had been shoved back into the wall, was a stapled manila folder. "Timberlake Matter" was lettered across the cover.

There was nothing inside the folder.

Ben kept it anyway and then searched the house again. He could find no trace of the photographs and notes H. J. had told him she'd seen.

He left the way he'd entered.

Sneaking into the garage, he searched it and the car. Neither Larry nor the missing notes on the Timberlake matter were there.

The unseen dog howled once more at Ben hurried to his car.

$\triangledown$

16

Ben had just hung up the phone, when it started ringing. Sitting again on his living-room sofa, he answered. "Spanner-Mavity residence."

"Well?" inquired H. J.'s voice.

"Are you all right?"

"Fit as a fiddle. I passed all my tests," she assured him.

"Where you calling from?"

"My hospital room. I have a private one. So tell me about Larry."

"All I can really tell you about is Larry's house," he explained and filled her in on what had happened.

"Somebody else obviously wants that material on the Timberlake heiress," she said, when he'd finished. "Might be the same person who followed me."

"Followed you when?"

"Oh, that's right, Ben. I haven't told you that I dropped in on Alicia Bertillion this afternoon. While I was driving over there I noticed that a—"

"Are you the same Helen Joanne Mavity who recently gave me her solemn word she'd wait for me before rushing off to grill people?"

"C'mon, you must know there's a time limit on my promises. I mean, when you decided to loiter in Manhattan, I figured I—"

"Who was following you?"

"Don't know. Somebody in a dirty Fiero. I succeeded in ditching them."

"Maybe," he said. "Are you certain, though, that it really was Larry who knocked you out?"

"Had to be him. You found the file folder at his house."

"The person in the Fiero could have conked you and then planted the folder there."

"Naw, too devious and complex. Besides I got a whiff of Larry's overpowering aftershave lotion just prior to being slugged," she said. "And, listen, that's what I must've smelled at Alicia's."

"He was there, too?"

"I didn't realize it at the time, but, yes, there was a trace of that distinctive Larry aroma lingering in the air," she explained. "I must be allergic to it, and I sneezed. Alicia saw him, Ben, and he was wearing a ski mask, just like—"

"Whoa. Rewind and explain. She *saw* Larry?"

"She came home and heard noises inside her house. She lives in this terrific converted barn with beamed—"

"I'm not in the market for a barn, so skip the real estate details. Tell me about Larry."

"That's exactly what I'm attempting to do, but you bitch about every touch of colorful description that I use. Anyway, she walked in on this big man who was searching her house. Quite obviously, hunting for Lloyd's file. This intruder was built like Larry and wore a ski mask and the same sort of dark outfit as the driver of the Audi that ran down Lloyd. He hit her, using a blackjack. Probably the same one he later used on me."

"How'd you get from her place to the old church?"

"Although Lloyd hadn't stored anything with her, he did tell her that he'd stashed something at St. Swithin's."

"Doggies, daughter," he said in his Gabby Hayes voice, "I can't make heads or tails out of this here yarn."

"The church on my *Love's Claimant* cover is called St. Swithin's in the novel, and I'm using, at Larry's suggestion, Brimstone Denominational as the model," she explained, a bit impatiently. "It occurred to me that their old graveyard would have been a neat place to hide something. I was right."

"But Larry tracked you there?"

"Right, exactly how I don't know. It was *after* I got a look at the stuff in the folder, though. Hey, have you phoned Juster to warn him?"

"Yep, I just tried. All I got was his answering tape. I told him to call collect as soon as he got the message, that it was an emergency."

"Dammit, if only we knew *her* name."

"This photographer will know. Soon as we connect with him, we—"

"Somebody may well be on the way there right now. Where is Willmur, anyway?"

"Few miles this side of Boston, small town."

"We aren't even sure who else is involved in this besides Larry. The Timberlakes or somebody else entirely."

"I'd bet on the Timberlakes."

"Why? Did Laura indicate that they—"

"Nope. But I ran into Larry on the train going in. I trailed him, and he went right to the Timberlake Building," he said. "Since Laura came to the lunch with me, he probably saw Don T. As I recall they're classmates."

"So who beat up Larry and stole the file stuff from him?"

"We don't know if that's what actually happened," he reminded her. "From what I know of Don Timberlake, though, he's not above doing that or, more likely, hiring someone."

"There could be others involved, non-Timberlakes."

"Such as who?"

She made a murmuring, shrugging sound. "I don't exactly know, Ben," she admitted. "Both Eva and old Oscar, however, seemed awfully curious about what, if anything, Lloyd might have confided in me before he died."

"Anybody who worked in the Dahlman Building could've found out that Lloyd was on the trail of the Timberlake baby."

H. J. said, "I just thought of something. If Larry went into New York when you did, could he have made it back here in time to ransack Alicia's?"

"When did that happen?"

"Around four."

"Sure, it's only an hour from Grand Central to Westport, usually," he answered. "Larry could've caught either the 1:07 or the 2:07. Oh, and he has a new version of his run yesterday."

"Different from what he told me?"

"The latest version has molasses in it."

"Okay, then, it was pretty certainly Larry who drove the stolen car that ran Lloyd down. The running stuff was his try at an alibi."

"He probably just ran as far as the spot where he'd hidden the car. Around here people don't pay much attention to joggers."

"Somehow—he was his assistant after all—Larry became aware of what Lloyd was digging in to," H. J. said thoughtfully. "But he figured you could make more money by selling the information to the Timberlakes. He knows Don T., and he assumed that the family might not want to rush right out and embrace the missing heiress. Maybe they aren't going to kill her, but they sure might want her to stay unaware of who she actually is."

"Lloyd wouldn't want that, though. To him this was probably the biggest story he'd ever run across, the stuff of bestsellers and media fame," said Ben. "He'd never agree to keep quiet, no matter what the bribe for silence. His ego was involved just as much as his bankbook."

"So Larry had to silence him."

"After which he had to gather up all the notes and pictures Lloyd was holding."

"Sure, so he went to all the women he knew his brother-

in-law was tied up with. He has to be the one who searched
my cottage, too."

"Yeah, you're right," she said. "Okay, we're all being really
clever. But how do we find out who actually has the
Timberlake material now?"

"We don't have to do that, H. J. We just have to get in
touch with this photographer Juster."

"But that's what they'll try to do."

"Yep, probably."

"I'm going to stay here tonight, but—"

"You bet your ass you're going to stay in the hospital."

"But, as I was about to say, first thing tomorrow we are
going to Willmur, Mass."

"I don't think that's necessary."

"I do. You keep trying Juster. I'm getting drowsy."

"I'll see you in the morning."

"I notice that you never say you love me anymore."

"I love you," he said in his Elmer Fudd voice and hung up.

Sankowitz appeared on Ben's doorstep just before eight the
next morning. "Oh, shit," he said when Ben opened the
door.

"And the same to you, my boy," he replied in his Barry
Fitzgerald voice. "What are you lamenting about?"

Dressed in a gray running suit, the cartoonist had a small
radio attached to his waistband and earphones on his head.
He pointed down at the radio. "I sometimes listen to the
news of the day as I dash along these rustic byways."

"Something bad about H. J.?"

"No, no, relax," he said, coming into the house. "But
close. She still in the hospital?"

"Yeah, I'm going to call her in an hour or so and see if
she's fit to come home. What did you hear on the news?"

"It's Larry Dalhman."

Ben had been returning to the kitchen and the coffee
maker. He stopped, frowning. "He's dead," he said.

"Right, you got it on the first guess."

He continued on into the kitchen. "Where'd they find him?"

"In his office at the Dahlman Building. Place had been ransacked, he'd been beaten, tortured, and then knifed. Very messy."

"Oh, shit." Ben sat at the butcher-block table.

"My exact reaction, as you may recall." Sankowitz poured himself a cup of coffee and then leaned against the sink. "This makes two people Helen was associated with who've met violent ends. The time has come to tell the police all you guys know and then retire to the sidelines."

"In many ways, Joe, she's like a boulder rolling down a hillside."

"She gathers no moss?"

"She's damn hard to stop."

"You better try. We're talking here about people who list murder among their job skills. They've already knocked off two—"

"No, we figure that Larry killed Dobkin. Someone else killed him."

"Huh?"

"I'll explain later." Getting up, he crossed to the wall phone and punched out a number.

"Brimstone General Hospital."

"Helen Joanne Mavity's room, please."

"One moment, sir."

"I hope you folks have Major Medical," said Sankowitz, sipping his coffee.

"I'm sorry, sir, Ms. Mavity is no longer a patient."

"What is she then?"

"She checked herself out."

"When was that?"

"An hour ago."

"Thanks." He hung up. "An hour ago—she should've gotten home by now."

"Not there, huh?"

"Never live with an independent woman."

"Too late now, you should've warned me earlier."

"H. J. says she'll wait until I call to come get her and then checks herself—"

The doorbell rang.

"This might be her." Ben hurried to the front door and opened it.

"I think we better have a talk," said Detective Ryerson of the Brimstone police.

$\triangledown$

17

RYERSON WAS A TALL, blond man, getting close to being
forty. The tan suit he was wearing had collected several
days' worth of wrinkles, especially at the elbows and knees.
"Is H. J. here?" he inquired as he entered Ben's living room.

"Expecting her at any moment. Like a cup of coffee?"

"I gave it up."

"Herb tea?"

"Nothing, thanks," said the police detective. "Why don't
we sit down?"

"Sure, fine." Ben took an armchair.

Sankowitz emerged from the kitchen. "Well, sir, I appre-
ciated this pit stop," he said. "I'll talk to you later, Ben. Heed
my advice, huh?" After nodding at the detective, he let himself out.

"What was he advising you about?"

"Stock market," answered Ben amiably.

Ryerson sat in a straight chair facing him. A multitude of
new wrinkles formed in his trouser legs. "You were more or
less helpful during that Kathcart business, Ben," he ac-
knowledged. "Your wife was something of a pain in the butt,
but it all worked out."

Ben nodded, striving to keep looking amiable and coop-
erative.

Ryerson continued, "Now we seem to be embarking together on another screwball murder case. I don't like these
kinds of cases; they give me, to be honest, stomach cramps."

"You're referring to Lloyd Dobkin's death?"

Ryerson held up his left hand. "Dobkin is run down, and
H. J. Mavity happens to be on the scene," he said, ticking
off a finger. "Then H. J. herself is assaulted in front of a
church that she isn't even a member of. Next Larry Dahlman
is killed, after being roughed up considerably. He, too, was
a sometimes business associate of your sometimes wife."

"Just coincidences."

The detective leaned forward. "What the hell is she up to
this time, Ben?"

"H. J. didn't actually cause any of this," he assured the
policeman. "It was purely by chance that she—"

The front door snapped open and H. J. came in. She had
a paisley scarf tied over her hair. "Detective Ryerson, how
nice to see you," she said sweetly. "It still is detective, isn't
it? You haven't been promoted to sergeant or inspector because of your brilliant handling of the Kathcart case?"

Ryerson stood up. "I dropped by the hospital this morning
to have a talk with you," he informed her. "You'd left."

Ben was watching her. "I thought I was scheduled to
transport you home."

"I took a cab because I wanted to pick up my car," she
explained, walking over to him. Bending, she kissed him on
the cheek and then sat on the sofa. "Did Ben offer you a cup
of coffee, Detective Ryerson?"

"I've given up coffee."

"How about a doughnut?"

"No, thanks." He sat again in the straightback chair.

"How about a waffle? I was thinking while I was driving
home that I'd love to have—"

"How's your head?" Ben asked her.

"Lovely." She touched the scarf. "Except they shaved a

patch of hair off me so they could stitch me up. I look sort of funny from the rear. I'll show you later. How about those waffles, Detective Ryerson?"

"No, thanks, H. J. What I'd like to do is ask you some questions."

"Fine." She leaned back on the sofa. "How about you, Ben? Waffle?"

"Already had breakfast."

Ryerson asked her, "Do you have any idea who hit you?"

She said, "Sure, it was Larry Dahlman."

"You actually saw him?"

"I smelled him, though I didn't get a look at him. I couldn't testify in court that it was Larry, but I know it was."

"He had a particular smell?"

Ben told her, "He's dead, H. J."

"I know. I saw it on the news while I was still in the hospital this morning."

"About this guy's odor?" persisted the policeman.

"Larry insisted on wearing a very strong and distinctive aftershave," she explained. "You couldn't miss that aroma."

"That's not much of an identification, but, okay, let's accept it for now," said the detective. "Why did he hit you?"

H. J. took a deep breath while looking from Ryerson to Ben and back to the policeman again. "I did a lot of thinking while I was lying there in my hospital bed," she said. "I'm aware, Detective Ryerson, that you consider me something of a nitwit. A spoiled suburban matron who pokes her nose into other people's business and makes a habit of withholding information."

"You have to admit that in the—"

"But from now on, especially in the light of what's happened to Larry Dahlman, I've made up my mind to tell you absolutely everything I know."

"That's smart."

Ben was watching her, and he noticed that she'd ceased looking in his direction. "Everything, H. J.?"

"Yes, the whole story as I've lived it," she answered, not

meeting his glance. "So, Ben you just keep mum and let me explain to your friend what's been going on."

"Go right ahead, dear." He started studying the distant ceiling.

H. J. toyed with the knot of her scarf. "I'm not one for giving the police advice on how to go about their business," she began. "But I think if you look into Larry's alleged alibi for the time of Lloyd's death, you'll be able to prove that he was lying. He didn't run five miles at all that day. Instead he probably only jogged to wherever it was he'd hidden that stolen car."

Ryerson straightened up. "You're saying Dahlman killed his brother-in-law?"

"That's it, yes."

"Then who killed him?"

"Well, there I can't help you, Detective Ryerson. I don't have the slightest notion," she replied. "And, since I'm washing my hands of this whole affair, you'll simply have to find that out for yourself."

"How about motive? Why, assuming that he actually did, would Dahlman kill Lloyd Dobkin?"

H. J. sighed, evidencing disappointment in herself. "All I can tell you is this," she said. "Lloyd had something Larry wanted. So he killed him and then started looking for it."

"Wouldn't it have been simpler to find it first and then kill him?"

"To a rational person such as yourself, of course. But I don't honestly believe that Larry—probably all those aftershave fumes affected his brain—was exactly rational."

Ryerson sat watching her for a moment. "Is that why Larry supposedly slugged you? Because he wasn't rational?"

"He must have thought I might have the object that he was hunting for," she suggested. "Because I was a friend of Lloyd's and had been with him the day he died."

"Uh huh." Ryerson got up, rubbing at a wrinkled elbow of his suit. "Now fill me in as to why you were at the Brimstone Denominational Church last night."

"That was Lloyd Dobkin's favorite church," she said. "I just wanted to say a prayer for him."

"I see. Larry just happened to be passing by?"

"I imagine he followed me."

"Do you know what this valuable object is?"

"All I know is that Lloyd mentioned he found something that was worth quite a bit. He was afraid people might attempt to swipe it from him."

"Can you guess what it might be, H. J.?"

She spread her hands and shrugged. "Nope. Sorry."

"I'll look into your suggestions." He started for the door.

Ben rose up and went along. "Let us know what you find out."

"Oh, I will," Ryerson promised. "I'm glad to see you up and around, H. J. Take care of yourself."

After Ben had shut the door, he went back to where H. J. was sitting. "Not a bad performance," he said. "You didn't convince him, but at least you muddied the waters."

"And I did it all without changing my voice once."

"Is your head really okay?"

"Seems to be functioning fairly well. Dr. McClennan looked me over from stem to stern this morning and pronounced me ready to return to my loved ones."

"Okay, what you better do now is rest and then—"

"Have you talked to Juster yet?"

"No luck." He shook his head. "I tried him twice more last night and then again this morning. All I get is the guy's tape. He's got a very nasal voice, by the way."

"Go pack a suitcase and we'll depart."

"For Willmur?"

"Where else?"

"Don't you want to have some waffles first?"

"You know I hate waffles," she said.

▽

18

Ben HANDLED THE DRIVING. By ten that morning they were traveling along the Merritt Parkway. The day was overcast.

H. J. had a small sketchbook open on her knee. "What did you just say?"

"That Sankowitz is probably right," he repeated. "We ought to notify the police."

"We did." She tapped her chin with her pencil and frowned down at what she was drawing. "We just had a cozy chat with Ryerson."

"The Willmur police are the ones I'm alluding to," he explained. "We should phone them now and—"

"And what?" She began drawing again. "We don't even know the woman's name."

"They can contact Juster."

"How? He's not answering his telephone."

"Well, they can go over to his place. Judging by the way he's listed in the Boston phone book, I'd guess it's his photo studio. Anyway, the cops rush there and warn him."

"Warn him about what?"

"That he's in danger. That the Timberlake baby is in danger."

H. J. produced a negative sound. "The police wouldn't

believe us if we told them that," she said. "I mean, we call them and say we have a hunch that the long-lost Timberlake heiress may be living right there in their own town. We know this because we happen to have a photo of a lady's bottom with a butterfly on it. Heck, they'd just wait until we pull into Willmur, and then toss a net over us."

"But we aren't going to reach there for another three hours at least. In that time all sorts of dire things could happen."

"Whoever took the stuff off Larry is probably already in Willmur."

"So why are we rushing?"

"We're not sure if Larry knew the woman's name or whether or not he told it to anyone," she said as she drew. "It could be our competition has to track down Juster, too, to find out where she is. It's possible we can still beat him to the prize."

"It's more likely they've found this damn photographer by now and persuaded him to tell all."

"That's possible."

"And once they find her, they'll probably knock her off."

"No, not yet."

"Why not?"

"Because they can't be certain that she is Sue Ellen Timberlake, for one thing. I'd want to establish that before I took the trouble of murdering someone," she told him. "For another, they don't know who else is aware of her existence. Maybe Lloyd told Juster about his theory, and maybe the photographer told the woman and lots of other people."

"And maybe they'll be having a ticker tape parade in her honor as we get there," he said. "But, in reality, we don't even know if Lloyd Dobkin ever got around to contacting Juster."

"Oh, I'm betting he did. I'm just uncertain as to how much he told the guy."

Ben concentrated on his driving for a moment. "I'm still not too clear about why Larry was killed."

"Several possibilities," she said. "To keep him quiet, first

off. Maybe once he told Timberlake what he knew, they figured it was best to silence him."

"The thing is, H. J., we also know just about everything
Larry Dahlman did."

"And we're probably on somebody's list," she said. "One
more reason to solve this mess quickly."

"One more reason to call the cops, rush home, dive into
bed, and pull the covers over our heads."

"She made a scornful noise. "There's another possible
reason for removing Larry. It could be somebody else was
aware of what he'd swiped and wanted the stuff for themselves."

"A free-lance hunter of missing heirs?"

"Lloyd may have hinted at his discovery to others besides
me," she said. "Larry may have confided in someone besides
Don T. Timberlake."

"What are you saying we have here—a Maltese Falcon
set-up? With various parties swiping the file from one another?"

"Sure, why not?"

"Larry knocks off Lloyd to eliminate the competition. He
takes the file after knocking you cold. But then someone
unknown—let's call him, oh, the Clutching Hand—this
Clutching Hand kills Larry to get hold of the stuff."

"Hey, I got a real bump on the head." She touched her
head through the scarf. "This isn't a matinee at the Bijou
we're attending, Ben."

"I'll attempt to be more serious in the future, Ms. Mavity," he assured her in his Richard Haydn voice.

"If there's no third party, then it's just the Timberlakes."
She was studying the drawing she'd made. Holding her pen-
cil in her teeth, she dug an eraser out of her shoulder bag.
"You still haven't told me all that you found out from Laura
Timberlake Barks."

"Not a hell of a lot," he admitted. "What's that you're
drawing, by the way?"

"Show you in a minute. Well, anything?"

"I mentioned to her that I'd seen Larry entering their building. Laura says he's a friend of her brother's, not hers."

"We already knew that."

Ben continued, "I did pick up one interesting item, though."

"Finally. What?"

"Laura swore me to secrecy, but there's apparently a plan afoot for Majutsu, Ltd., the immense Japanese concern, to buy the Timberlake set-up."

She glanced over at him. "So?"

"Though I'm not exactly an expert on world finance, it seems to me that if another Timberlake were to appear right now and cause a big legal frumus over who really owns what . . . well, it might just futz up this whole Majutsu deal."

She nodded. "More reason for the Timberlakes to suppress this whole business."

"Reason to suppress, but is it reason for bumping off people?"

"We're talking about millions of dollars here, are we not?"

"Yup. Could be billions."

"That's sufficient motive then." She added a few new lines to the drawing. "As soon as we pass this clunky Subaru in front of us, I want to show something."

"I wasn't planning to pass it."

"They're doing less than fifty. We don't want to be stuck behind them from here to Hartford."

"Okay, okay." He glanced at the mirrors in turn, then eased around the slow-moving car ahead of them.

"You can go faster than fifty-five yourself, you know. They rarely give tickets unless you're doing over—-"

"Show me what you were going to show me."

"Take a quick look." She held up the sketch. "This is Sue Ellen Timberlake."

Ben took a quick look. "Only her head."

"Sufficient for identification purposes."

"She's pretty, and there is a slight resemblance to Laura."

"I had a chance to study all the photographs before they were swiped from me. I'm certain that this is a good likeness of the woman in those pictures."

"Could come in handy."

Taking a porous-point pen from her bag, she commenced inking the pencil drawing. "If we can't find Juster, we can schlep this around to various places."

"Such as?"

"Oh, places where people go all the time. The post office, churches, the library."

"Do skin models frequent the library?"

"Just because a woman poses naked doesn't mean she's a dimwit," said H. J. "I remember my father telling me once that—"

"Whoa, halt," he warned. "I really don't want to talk about your father."

Snapping shut the sketchbook, she dropped it and the pen into her bag. "Then we won't talk about anything." She folded her arms and started glowering out at the highway.

After seven or eight quiet miles, just before they reached the tunnel in New Haven, Ben said, "Okay, talk about your father."

H. J. continued to stare out at the overcast morning. She did not speak.

"You're aware that I never liked him," Ben said after another mile and a half. "And, lord knows, he sure didn't like me."

"He thought you were very gifted," she mentioned finally, her voice a shade hoarse.

"Did he? That's news to me," said Ben, hunching his shoulders slightly as they entered the tunnel. "All he ever called me to my face was 'asshole.' "

"He only did that when he'd been drinking."

"Your father was always drinking. He kept himself marinated, from the inside, every hour of the day and night."

"All right, okay, my father was an alcoholic," she admitted

as their car emerged from the tunnel and into the grayness of the day. "That doesn't mean he wasn't fond of you."

Ben shook his head. "We really can't seem to talk about him," he told her. "What I mean is, I saw Edwin Mavity not simply as an alcoholic, but as a vicious drunk. He used to hit you when you were a kid, your sister, too. He tried to take a sock at me on several memorable—"

"You just never got to see the gentle side of him."

"True, hey, that's true. 'What did you do to my daughter this time, asshole?' Nope, that wasn't his gentle side."

"Don't."

"Don't what?"

"Do his voice."

"Was I?"

"Yes, but please, don't." She still wasn't looking his way. "My father really was a very good illustrator. His tragedy was he happened to get started when magazine illustration was going down the chutes. Eventually he had to leave commercial art altogether."

"I'm aware you think you inherited all your talent from him," said Ben. "Honestly, though, he wasn't an especially good artist."

"Acting is your specialty," she reminded him. "I think I can judge drawing ability better than you. My father was an exceptional artist."

"I've looked at the stuff in that old portfolio of his, remember? He was just passable."

"I suppose that's how you'd sum up my work, too."

"Nope, you're terrific."

"Oh, yes. Which is why I'm painting an endless procession of bimbos with their tits spilling out of their gowns."

"Not as of now," he reminded. "You've just changed careers in midstream."

"I'll probably end up like my father."

"No comment."

"That was really so stupid, the way he died. Getting run down by a taxi."

"Lots of people get hit by cabs in Manhattan."

"But not a heck of a lot of them while staggering out of a bar."

"Quite a few probably."

"Shit," she said, folding her hands in her lap.

"You weren't anywhere near P. J. Malley's Saloon that night nine years ago," he told her. "There was nothing you could've done."

"I should have tried harder to persuade him to get help for his drinking problem."

"You did try that, many a time."

"Yes, but I could never get him to go. He'd promise and promise and then—"

"Over," Ben said. "It's over a long time."

"And now Lloyd. I couldn't save his life, either."

"Despite what your dear old dad taught you, your primary purpose in life isn't to look after middle-aged men who've screwed up their lives."

Shaking her head slowly, she leaned back in the seat. "Wake me when we hit the Massachusetts border," she requested, shutting her eyes.

▽

19

T HE SHOP OF "Mark Juster, Photographer," was on a twisting, tree-lined lane off the main street of the small town of
Willmur. On its left stood Macri's Grocery, a defunct mom-
and-pop that looked to have shut down many months before.
On the right was a wine shop calling itself It's a Grape Life.

The overcast sky had gradually faded, and when Ben and
H. J. left their parked car to cross the street, the sun was
shining thinly up in the midday sky.

"Business isn't exactly thriving in these parts," remarked
H. J.

The shade was down on the photographer's glass door and
a dangling sign announced "Sorry, We're Closed."

"You're sorry?" said Ben in his Sylvester voice. "You're
sorry?"

H. J. was scanning the narrow display window, which had
several small posters taped to it. Inside were arranged nine
starkly framed photos. "Not a single shot of the lady we're
hunting for."

After a careful glance around, Ben took hold of the knob.
It turned and he shoved the door slowly open. "Let's take a
look inside," he suggested.

"Door wasn't locked?"

"Nope." He stood on the threshold of the shadowy shop, listening.

"That's usually a bad sign." She nudged him inside and followed.

Ben quietly shut the door. "In this case, a sign that somebody preceded us."

They were in an office-reception room. The drawers of the row of black filing cabinets against the gray wall had all been yanked open. Folders lay spilled on the white carpeting, along with envelopes that were leaking negatives, an assortment of business letters, dozens of glossy photos, and wads of memo slips.

"Larry Dahlman couldn't be responsible for this one," H. J. observed. "He's dead."

"This must be the handiwork of his successor."

"Okay, then we can conclude that this successor didn't know the model's name or address. Came here and broke in and hoped to find out." She roamed the room as she spoke, picking up scattered photos at random and glancing at them. "He shot other nudes besides ours."

"There are a couple things I'm curious about." Ben sat at the white desk. "Did whoever did this job actually get to talk to Juster? And does he have the Timberlake baby's current address?"

"Well, whatever the answers may be, Ben, it isn't likely we're going to find any information on her whereabouts here. Too late."

Ben had noticed the top sheet of the memo pad beside the gray phone. "That's interesting."

"What?"

"Phone number scribbled here looks vaguely familiar. I'd guess that Juster wrote it and not our ransacker," he told her. "A New York City number." Picking up the phone, he punched out the number.

After three rings a recorded voice answered. "Good afternoon, this is Timberlake Products. If you wish our Executive Department, punch one. If you wish—"

Nodding, Ben hung up. "Timberlake headquarters in far-off Manhattan."

"You think Juster called Don T. Timberlake?" Stepping over the scatter of photos and files, H. J. approached the desk.

"He must've called somebody there. Of course, it could be he just wanted to buy a box of soap."

"How the heck did he know about—holy cow!" She was looking beyond him now, at the single black bookshelf on the wall behind the desk. Reaching over, she snatched a book from among the seven displayed there. "Here's another interesting item."

Smiling, she handed him a copy of Lloyd Dobkin's *Great American Kidnappings.* "The bookmark," he said, "is at the picture of the Timberlake baby."

"So this guy knows who she is."

"Who she *might* be."

"I'd truly love to know at what point in the proceedings he found out."

Ben stood. "We may as well depart, before any cops wander in here."

H. J. dropped the book into her shoulder bag. "That makes two copies I'm hefting."

They were able to get back out on the sidewalk without being noticed.

H. J. stepped over for a final inspection of the photographer's window. "Hey, look at this." She pointed at one of the posters.

It announced an upcoming series of performances of the classic mystery play *13 Guests at Darkwood Inn.* There were five cast members listed—Carolyn Wyler, Klaus North, Nancy Marschall, J. P. Marquis, and Mark Juster.

H. J. tapped the window. "A model might also be interested in acting."

"Many are," he said. "We'd best drop in at the Willmur Community Theatre and show your sketch around."

"First I want to buy a bottle of wine."

"Wine? We have a sufficient supply at home."

"Sure, but I'd also like to talk to Juster's next-door neighbor," she said.

"Can you drive and sulk at the same time?" H. J. asked.

"Yep, I've had considerable practice."

They were on Willmur's main thoroughfare again, heading for the community theater.

"You're a nitwit," she remarked after a while.

"Probably so."

"Anyway, I *wasn't* flirting with him."

"Fine."

"However, being sweet and amiable is one of the tried and true techniques of interrogation."

"Right. Jack Webb did a lot of that on *Dragnet.*"

"Plus which, the proprietor of It's a Grape Life is an elderly man."

"Fifty."

"Too old for me."

"What's your cut-off age?"

"And, thanks to me, we found out some valuable things."

"Telling the guy you thought his wine shop had a cute name. Jesus."

"Lying is another sure-fire tool in questioning people."

"As is holding hands?"

"I didn't hold his hand, Ben. I simply lingered over the handshake."

"Ten minutes. That must be the world's record for lingering."

"He had some useful information for us. For instance we now know what Juster looks like. He's a tall, rawboned man with a dark beard."

"Description also fits Abe Lincoln."

"And we know Juster hasn't been at his photo shop since Tuesday morning. That's *after* Lloyd was killed."

"You figure Juster went into hiding when he heard about Dobkin?"

"Seems a possibility. Have you quite sulking?"

"Not completely, no, but I'm thawing."

"Bob doesn't know Juster's home address, and there's nothing but his shop address in the phone book. We have to find out where the guy resides."

"Bob?"

"Bob Webster, the proprietor of It's a Grape Life."

"I was hoping he'd be able to identify the girl in the sketch."

"That was disappointing, yes. He never saw anyone looking like her with Juster, doesn't know who she could be."

"Since he didn't hear any noise next door, we can assume the burglar must've hit during the night."

"Probably drove right up here to Willmur soon as he killed Larry Dahlman."

"Unless he was already here."

"Meaning there's more than one person hunting for the heiress?"

"Could be a whole team."

"We want to turn on Quincy Street, don't we?"

"Yes."

"That was Quincy Street you just drove by."

Lightning flashed and thunder rumbled, hard rain pelted the leaded windows of the old country inn. The two wall lamps that feebly illuminated the dark, hollow lobby flickered and nearly died.

The slim, blond young woman who was standing fearfully in the exact center of the polar bear rug was alone on the stage of the Willmur Community Theatre. She brought one trembling hand up to her mouth as the handle on the heavy wooden door began rattling.

The handle slowly turned, and the door swung inward with much creaking.

The young woman gasped, taking a frightened step backward.

A grizzled old man in a faded mackinaw, faded jeans, and heavy boots came staggering in out of the stormy night.

"Jeb, what's wrong?" asked the young woman.

"It's . . . it's . . . the thirteenth guest," he muttered in a New England voice and then fell face down at her feet.

"Terrible accent," whispered Ben.

"Hush," advised H. J.

They were standing at the back of the small theater, surrounded by dark empty seats.

There was an ax buried in the rustic caretaker's back.

The blond noticed it and screamed.

A handsome young man in white sweater and white trousers came bounding into the room from stage left. "Hazel, dearest, whatever's wrong?"

"It's . . . Jeb," she sobbed, pointing at the fallen man with a quivering finger. "And, oh, Leon, there's a hatchet protruding from his back."

"So there is." Striding over, Leon knelt beside the body. "Poor fellow. I fear he's dead, Hazel."

"Oh, Leon, who will be next?" asked Hazel and fainted.

The curtain fell.

As the house lights came up, a lean bald man of about sixty rose from a second-row seat. "Not too bad," he called. "We'll run through the next act in ten minutes, gang."

Catching hold of Ben's arm, H. J. hurried him down the slanting aisle. "Excuse me," she called to the bald man. "Are you Jack Fullerton?" His name had been on the poster, too.

"Afraid so." He turned, studying them as they approached.

"You seem to be doing a marvelous job of directing," she told him, smiling sweetly.

"Well, thanks, ma'am. Who are you, by the way?"

"I'm H. J. Mavity," she explained. "This is Ben Spanner."

Fullerton grinned, and his eyes widened for an instant. "The voice man?"

"Yep," admitted Ben.

"I was with a Boston ad agency for nine ungodly years. I think we used you at least once. On some Shawn's Sparkling Cider commercials maybe?"

"Right. I was the sour apple."

"Would you have time to talk to the guy who's playing Jeb? His Down East dialect sucks."

"Actually," put in H. J., "we're here on my account. See, Mark Juster was supposed to provide me with some photos for a rush paperback cover I'm painting. But he seems to have disappeared from his place of business. Since we knew he's in your play, I'm hoping he's around here someplace."

Fullerton shook his head. "He's not here, and I don't know where the hell he is," he told her. "He's playing Ace Ricardo, an important part, and I've been using a sub who's nowhere near as good."

Ben asked, "When's the last time you saw him?"

"We have two sorts of actors in this thing." The director sat on the arm of an aisle seat. "People who can come to afternoon rehearsals and those who have jobs and can only hit the night sessions. Mark only came evenings, and the last time he showed was on Monday."

"Any explanation?"

"Nothing. Not a damn word from him since."

H. J. asked, "Have you tried his home?"

"You know, I don't know where Mark lives. I always got in touch with him through his photo shop."

Ben said, "Is that Juster's usual pattern, to go off without a word?"

"No, he's usually very dependable. You see, he also does all our publicity photos and he doesn't want to make anybody mad."

From her bag H. J. took the sketch. "I'm especially anxious to find this particular model," she told him. "Is she a member of your cast?"

He scanned the picture. "Wish she was," he said, grinning and handing it back.

"Well, do you know who she is?" persisted H. J. "Juster gave me the impression she was a close friend of his."

"She might be," said Fullerton. "But I haven't any notion who the lady is."

$\bigtriangledown$

20

THEY STARTED BACK UP the theater aisle. Then H. J. stopped in her tracks, snapped her fingers, and said, "Of course."

"Eh?" said Ben.

"I never forget a face. C'mon." She led him back the way they'd come. "Mr. Fullerton, what's the name of the woman playing Hazel?"

"That's Carolyn Wyler. You thinking of using her as a model instead?"

"Never can tell. Might we talk with her?"

"Sure, she's backstage someplace. Use that door yonder." He pointed at an exit.

Carolyn was sitting, legs up, on a prop sofa. She was smoking a cigarette and going over a copy of the play. " 'But, Leon, I did . . . I saw a face at the *window.*' No, shit. 'I saw a *face* at the window.' "

"I *saw* a face at the window," offered Ben as they halted next to the flowered sofa.

"You think so?" she asked, looking up at him and exhaling smoke.

He nodded. "Sure, because Leon is the kind of dimwit who never believes the obvious. You're trying to convince him that you really did *see* something. An escaped lunatic, in fact, and the man who'll turn out to be the thirteenth guest."

"You familiar with this stupid play?"

"Played in it in high school."

"In what role?"

"Jeb."

"Really? I'd think you'd be a perfect Leon. Not that you're a dimwit, but because you're obviously the leading man type."

"Thanks, but Leon's a wimp. Character parts are the most fun in—"

"Mightn't we get on to business?" interrupted H. J.

"I'm not really sure what business is," admitted Ben. "So I've been indulging in a little light badinage."

H. J. looked at the blond actress. "You've posed for Mark Juster, haven't you?"

"A few times. Why are you—"

"I saw her photo on the floor," she said to Ben.

"Ah," he said.

Turning to Carolyn, H. J. said, "I'm a painter. I do paperback covers and—"

"You call that painting?" asked the young woman. "I'd think in order to call yourself a painter you'd have to do *serious* work. Museum stuff."

"Okay, I'm a commercial artist," said H. J., fists starting to clench slightly. "The point is, dear, that I'm anxious to contact Mark. He was supposed to do some photos for me."

"Don't tell me you posed for him?" She sat up, planting her feet on the floor. "It's tough for an older woman to get anywhere in the men's mag field. Too many wrinkles and bulges, which turn off the—"

"I'm thirty-two—no, thirty-one until next week," H. J. told her. "I'm not old and I don't bulge or sag or—"

"That's true," said Ben. "Carolyn, do you know where we can find Juster?"

"No, not really. But you might try his sister."

"Sister?"

"Her name's Linda Albright, and she lives across town on Emerson Lane," said the actress. "Mark more or less lives there, when he's not shacked up with someone."

H. J. produced her sketch. "Do you know who this is?"

Taking the drawing, Carolyn replied, "Well, this isn't a very good likeness, but it could be Mardy."

"Not a good likeness?" said H. J., snatching it back. "Hell, it's—"

"Who's Mardy?" asked Ben. "What's her full name?"

"I don't know. I saw her with Mark once or twice. Mardy . . . no, I can't remember."

"How recently did you see her with him?"

"Oh, a couple weeks ago."

"Where?"

"It was probably at the Bunker Hill Café. That's one of his favorite hangouts. I'm not certain, though."

"Do you know what she does, where she works?"

"Sorry, no," replied the actress. "Could you drop by later to help me go over these lines?"

"I'd like to, except—"

"We have to go." H. J. took hold of Ben's nearest arm and tugged.

"It'll work," Ben assured her while parking down the block from the house of Mark Juster's sister.

"My system's been working." She climbed out of the car, stretched.

"Some people like to be helpful, some don't," he pointed out, joining her on the cracked sidewalk. "But everybody likes the idea of potential money."

"Okay, we'll give your way a try. What's my name during this scam?"

"Miss Mavity."

"Very inventive."

"And I'm Prentiss Choate."

"I don't doubt it."

The house they wanted was a narrow two-story one of pale red brick. Instead of a lawn, there was a small stretch of green-tinted cement.

When Ben pushed the bell, cats commenced yowling inside.

"Quiet, please. Quiet," someone said inside. "This is no way to act."

The cats, three or four of them at least, continued to howl.

"Yes?" A thin, gray-haired woman opened the door a few inches.

"Linda Albright?" inquired Ben in his Boston voice.

"William Buckley," murmured H. J. into her fist.

"Yes. And you are . . . ?"

Holding out his hand, he smiled falsely. "Prentiss Choate of Healy and Associates."

"I don't believe I'm familiar with that name."

"Second largest advertising agency in the Boston area—in the whole blooming state, for that matter," he amplified. "We rushed over here from Boston—this is Miss Mavity, my personal secretary—to contact your—"

"She's quite pretty."

"Thank you," said H. J.

"We'd like to contact your—"

"Bad boy. Mustn't do that, Kafka." She reached down and caught a pudgy black cat by the scruff of his neck and thwarted his attempt to escape out into the afternoon. "You're very naughty."

"What Mr. Choate is trying to explain," put in H. J., "is that we have a very important advertising assignment for your brother. Is he at home?"

"Go sit by Dos Passos." She set the cat on the hallway floor, propelling him toward the living room with a pat on the backside. "Scoot now, you hear?"

"Your brother," said Ben, "is he here?"

"No, I'm sorry, he isn't."

"Can you tell us where to reach him?"

She hesitated before answering, "I can't really."

H. J. said, "We understood that he lives with you."

"Quite a lot of the time he does. Just now, though, he's off on a job someplace or other."

"Where exactly?"

"I'm not really certain, Mr. Choate," she admitted. "I know he told me he was going out of town for a few days to shoot some pictures, but I'm nearly sure he didn't say where."

H. J. said, "How much did you say you were prepared to pay him, Mr. Choate?"

"In the neighborhood of fifty thousand dollars, Miss Mavity."

"Fifty thousand dollars?" asked Linda Albright. "Mark could actually earn that much on one assignment?"

"Only if we can find the man at once," explained Ben. "Otherwise, because of a very tight deadline, we'll have to use our second choice. That would mean no fifty thousand for your brother and, probably, no future assignments from Healy and Associates."

"What account is it for?"

"Sunskin Swimwear."

"That's a very good company. Some years ago I bought myself a Sunskin—"

"Is your brother likely to phone you while he's away?" asked H. J.

"Sometimes he does, there's no way of telling. Mark has always been extremely independent."

"Well, should he phone, please tell him that Mr. Choate of Healy and Associates is extremely anxious to get in touch with him. Get a number where we can reach him."

"Where can he contact you?" asked his sister.

"We won't be back at the Boston office until quite late this evening probably," Ben told her. "You'd better give me your number here, and I'll call you later on to see if you've heard from him."

She provided the phone number, adding, "I'm certain Mark will do a better job for you than your second choice."

From her shoulder bag H. J. extracted the drawing. "We're also anxious to contact this model," she said. "Do you know who she is?"

The woman looked at the picture, then brightened. "Oh, yes, of course. That's Mardy Cranford."

$\triangledown$

21

THE ROHMER REALTY OFFICES were housed in a vine-covered cottage with strawberry-colored shutters. The tiny parking lot was bordered with a profusion of bright multi-colored flowers, and a small, flat wooden pig had been set up on the square of grass beside the path leading to the red-painted door.

"I wonder if all seven of the dwarfs are home." Ben slid out of the car.

H. J. said, "I think it's a very cute little office."

"For somebody who's lying in wait for Hansel and Gretel maybe."

Walking beside him, she asked, "Are you really going to be Prentiss Choate again?"

"Not if Mardy Cranford herself is here. Then we'll just try a sanitized version of the truth."

"That Buckley voice of yours gives me the willies."

"It's more a Kennedy voice, with a touch of Jim Backus." Taking hold of the gold doorknob, he opened the door of the real estate office and they walked in.

"I think I have just what you're looking for." A heavyset blond woman in a somewhat Hawaiian dress popped up from behind one of the three small desks.

There was no one else in the office.

H. J. explained, "We're looking for Mardy Cranford."

"Then you're not the Kupperbergs?"

"Haven't been for ages," H. J. assured her. "Is Mardy around?"

"Isn't that funny," observed the plump realtor, shaking her head. "That young lady is certainly getting popular."

"Has someone else been asking after her?" Ben inquired in his Choate voice. "It looks as though we might have competition, eh, Ms. Mavity?"

"My, yes, doesn't it." Smiling at the woman, H. J. asked her, "Who else is interested in her?"

"An attorney, he said he was."

"Attorney?" Ben took a few steps toward her desk. "What'd he look like?"

"Very Nordic."

"We're most anxious to talk to Mardy about some photographs her friend Mark Juster took of her," H. J. said. "Do you happen to know where we might find her?"

"Isn't that, now, a coincidence? The lawyer showed me a photo of Mardy. Well, not a complete photo, only her head snipped from a larger picture."

"The file," murmured H. J., nudging Ben.

"How long ago was this attorney here?"

"Oh, not more than a half hour ago. I'd just come back to the office after showing the Nolan House to a lovely young couple who're relocating from Nesbit Ferry, Georgia, and he was—"

"Did you send the guy to where Mardy is?"

The realtor nodded. "Yes, he had a check for her for the settlement of a claim she—"

"Where is she?" asked H. J.

"Oh, at the Shatsworth mansion. We've been asked by the owners to supervise some renovations, and Mardy is spending the afternoon there taking notes and measuring—"

"Where is this place?"

"I'll draw you a detailed map."

"A quick sketch will do," said H. J.

⋆   ⋆   ⋆

As he backed the car out of the real estate parking lot, Ben said, "Who's the lad pretending to be a lawyer?"

"Could Don T. Timberlake pass for a Scandinavian?" She was holding the penciled map on her knee.

"No, there aren't too many short, dark Nordics."

"Well, it can't be Mark Juster. Turn left at this next corner," she instructed. "Juster is allegedly Lincolnesque."

"I don't think there's a real attorney involved in this yet."

"Seems unlikely," H. J. agreed. "Although it's just possible the Timberlakes have dispatched somebody to check out Mardy."

He made the left turn. "We're not certain they know how to contact her directly."

"Take a right at the antique shop. Juster could've told them."

"He'd be more likely to hold out that information."

"But maybe he phoned them, after he found out that Lloyd had been killed. You know, offered to sell them news of a possible Timberlake heiress."

"You're assuming the guy is a scoundrel and a cad."

"Fellows who snap pictures of their girlfriends jaybird naked are most usually schmucks and not especially trustworthy," she observed. "So I don't believe he called the Timberlakes in Manhattan simply to pass on the glad news that their missing cousin was still alive."

"Yeah, but that doesn't mean he's sold her out. He could just be trying to negotiate with them on her behalf."

"Naw, he hasn't even told her that she's a potential heiress."

"How do you know that?"

"Okay, *he* has to have a pretty clear idea who she is, because we know he's read a copy of Lloyd's book," she said, tapping her forefinger on the map. "But she doesn't know she's a Timberlake, because she's still working for that real estate outfit."

"Some people don't quit their jobs even after inheriting millions or hitting the lottery or—"

"Hooey. Go around this upcoming circle and take the street that goes by that quaint ice-cream parlor. Wingert Road."

Ben did. "I was thinking," he said. "This 'attorney' must have the Timberlake file that Larry Dahlman swiped from you."

"I already told you that, ninny."

"When?"

"Back there."

"I didn't hear you. The point is, the lad who has that folder and the pictures of Mardy—he's a strong contender for the part of Larry's murderer."

"And right now he's probably with Mardy, alone in an old dark house," she said. "That must be the reservoir over there."

"That big hole with the water in it, you mean?"

"All right, take the first left after we pass it."

"I'm still not crystal clear about who's doing what to whom," Ben admitted.

"Larry Dahlman killed Lloyd Dobkin. That much we know for sure."

"Yeah, but after that it gets mighty fuzzy."

"There's the stone wall. Boy, spikes along the top and all," she said, pointing. "The gate should be right along—yes, there it is."

Ben drove onto the overgrown grounds of the Shatsworth estate. There were several acres of woods and brush surrounding the house. It rose up at the end of a long curving drive, a three-story Victorian mansion. Pale gray, all its windows were shuttered, and its vast lawn was rich with high weeds and wildflowers.

A blue station wagon was parked in front of the rickety multicar garage. And close behind it a dusty black Fiero.

"Ben, hey, that's the car that followed me the other day." H. J. hopped out of the car as he stopped.

"You sure?"

"Of course, because I recognize the—"

From inside the house came a scream and then a shot.

▽

22

THE CARVED WOODEN FRONT door of the mansion had been wedged open with a doorstop. Voices were drifting out of the old house into the gray afternoon as H. J. and Ben cautiously climbed the front steps.

"I didn't mean for that to happen, Miss Cranford," a man was apologizing.

"I *am* going to call the police."

"No, I can't let you do that."

H. J. whispered, "I know who that is."

"The guy, you mean?"

Nodding, she replied, "Yes, that's Bjornsen."

"Who's Bjornsen?"

"You know, old Mr. Dahlman's driver."

"What's he doing here in the wilds of Massachusetts?"

"We'd better find out."

"I don't imagine the venerable old gent is with him," said Ben. "Wait here."

"Don't get too tricky," she warned.

Ben went doddering, loudly, up the remaining steps. There was no one visible in the long, musty hallway. He grabbed the brass knocker, whapped the open door with it several times. "Bjornsen, you idiot!" he yelled into the house in his old man Dahlman voice. "I want you to drop that gun at once. Drop it, do you hear me?"

Five seconds passed.

Then came a thunk.

It sounded very much like a gun hitting the hardwood floor. Ben hurried into the house.

The thud had come from the first room on the left. He looked in through the beaded curtain.

A .38 revolver lay near the empty stone fireplace. A large blond man in a too-tight blue suit was standing wide-legged in front of the candy-striped love seat, facing a slim blond young woman, pale, one hand touching her throat.

Ben went diving into the room. He scooped up the gun and turned to point it at the big chauffeur. "What the hell is going on?"

"Where's Mr. Dahlman?" inquired the perplexed Bjornsen. "I didn't think he even knew where I was."

"You're Mardy Cranford?" Ben asked the young woman without glancing at her.

"Yes," she said, nodding. "Do you have any notion of what this is all about?"

"Some, yeah."

"Well, good afternoon, Bjornsen." Smiling, H. J. entered the parlor.

"Miss Mavity?" He blinked. "Did you bring Mr. Dahlman with you?"

"Actually we hoaxed you." She walked over to the love seat to pick up the briefcase that was lying there.

"My husband is a voice man."

"A what, miss?"

"An actor," amplified Ben. "Sit yourself down on that seat, Bjornsen."

"Mr. Dahlman's not out in the hall then?" He sat, sagging some. "For all he knows I really am off visiting my sick sister over in Long Island?"

"Quite probably." H. J. was poking around in the briefcase. "Here's the Timberlake folder, Ben."

Mardy cleared her throat. "Would you people mind if I asked who you were?'

"I'm Ben Spanner. This is H. J. Mavity."

The blond didn't lose her frown. "Somehow I don't feel any further along than I was."

"First fill us in on what Bjornsen was up to."

"Well, he told me he was an attorney named Wolverton and that he wanted me to come and talk with his client about a matter of great importance to me," she explained. "I don't know—he didn't look like either a lawyer or a Wolverton. So I suggested that he please leave. When he refused, I started for the phone over there to call the police. That's when he pulled the gun out of his briefcase."

"I didn't mean for it to go off," insisted the chauffeur. "But she pushed me, and I pulled the trigger by mistake. My orders are not to hurt anyone—not seriously anyway."

H. J. was leafing through the contents of the folder. "Orders from who?"

"I'd rather not say, Miss."

"C'mon, say." Ben gestured at him with the .38.

Bjornsen twisted the suit fabric at his knee with blunt fingers and studied the floor. "Well, it's Eva."

"Eva Dahlman Dobkin?" H. J. looked up from the folder. "Lloyd Dobkin's widow, huh."

"She and I," explained Bjornsen, blushing, "are . . . well, you know, friends."

"Where is she?"

"At the General Willmur Inn here in town, waiting for me to bring the young lady to her."

"What's Eva want with her?"

He fiddled with the fabric of his suit again. "Book rights, magazine serial rights, possibly a finder's fee. Things of that sort, miss."

H. J. smiled. "Eva wants to take over where Lloyd left off."

"Book rights, magazine rights," said the perplexed Mardy. "What does any of that have to do with me?"

"You don't know, do you?" said H. J.

"No, I don't have any idea of what you people are talking about."

Ben made a wait-a-minute gesture at her. To Bjornsen he said, "You're working for Eva, you say."

"Yes, I'm helping her, sir."

"That means she had you kill her own brother."

The driver jumped to his feet, shaking his head vigorously. "No, no," he told them. "I took that file, surely. But I never killed Larry Dahlman."

$\triangledown$

23

THEY'D PERSUADED THE BIG chauffeur to reseat himself.

Ben was sitting in a rickety straightback chair facing him. "You'd better explain a bit more," he suggested, the revolver resting on his knee.

"Eva came up with the idea, oh, a week or more ago, that her husband was up to something," Bjornsen began. "Not another woman thing—she was used to those. 'That little prick'—you'll pardon my language, ladies—'That little prick is up to something, Dean.' That's my first name. Dean. She suggested I start tailing him to—"

"Did you try to kill him?" H. J. was standing, arms folded, in front of the dead fireplace. "By draining the fluid out of—"

"We never tried to kill anyone, miss. You have to believe that."

"Go on," urged Ben.

"After Mr. Dobkin was run down, Eva was more certain than ever that he'd been on to something lucrative," Bjornsen continued. "She had me follow various people, to see if they knew anything or if he'd left any notes or other material with them."

"You followed me," said H. J.

"A couple of times, miss, yes, but then she told me to stick with Larry. Somehow, she'd begun to suspect that he knew something."

"You were following him the night he slugged me."

"I was, miss, and I'm very sorry I couldn't stop to help out. My orders, though, were to stay with him."

Ben said, "You followed him home, took the file."

"Yes, I did," admitted Bjornsen. "I knew it must be important or he wouldn't have hurt Miss Mavity in order to obtain it."

"Did you and Larry fight over possession?"

"That wasn't necessary. I was able to sneak up on him, tap him twice on the skull. He never even saw me."

"This all took place at Larry's house?"

"That's right. I left him lying in his living room unconscious and took the folder back to Eva."

From the armchair where she was restlessly listening, Mardy asked, "Is this all going to have something to do with me eventually?"

"Very much so," promised H. J.

"When Eva went through the notes and the photographs," Bjornsen said, "she put it all together. 'The little prick was on to a million-dollar yarn here, Dean.' We tried to phone Juster, but weren't able to contact him directly. Then we decided we better drive up here."

"Did you ever find Juster?"

"No, sir. So we took her photos—just the head, since you can't flash nudes around—and showed them at the library, churches, and the post office. That, eventually, got us an identification."

"Told you that would work," H. J. said to Ben.

Slowly Mardy stood. "This has something to do with those stupid pictures that Mark talked me into posing for, doesn't it?"

"It surely does," H. J. assured her.

The chauffeur said, "You have to understand that Eva and I haven't really done anything seriously wrong. There's really no need to take any legal action against us."

"Breaking and entering, assault," listed Ben, "threatening people with a gun. Bjornsen, I'm really going to have to turn you over to the cops."

"That would ruin Miss Mavity's chances of ever selling anything to Dahlman's publications again."

H. J. laughed. "I'll risk that."

"No!" Suddenly Bjornsen lunged at Ben, shoving at him with both hands.

The ancient chair toppled over backward and Ben went falling. He smacked the stones of the fireplace with the side of his head.

There was a brief show of jagged specks of colored light. Profound darkness followed.

Ben produced a grunting sound.

He became aware that the right side of his face was considerably colder than the left. Furthermore, his right knee and his right elbow felt funny.

Grunting again, he opened his eyes.

He found himself staring at a pair of large black dress shoes. The shoes had feet in them.

Taking a couple of deep breaths, he started pushing himself up off the stone floor in front of the parlor fireplace. "Is that me?"

Someone was breathing loudly in an odd, snoring way.

"Nope, it's not me. It's Bjornsen."

The chauffeur was sprawled on his back, feet pointing at the empty fireplace. He was unconscious, breathing in and out in a hoarse, grating way through his open mouth.

Neither H. J. nor Mardy was in the room.

"Bjornsen." Ben knelt, giving the man's shoulder a few shakes. "Dean? What happened here?"

The big man went on snoring.

There was, Ben noticed now, a large, discolored lump over Bjornsen's left ear.

"Somebody slugged him." Ben stood again. "H. J.?" he called out, his voice still a shade rusty.

There was no answer.

"Okay, I hit my head when he shoved me over." Ben glanced around the parlor. The gun that he'd been holding was gone and so was the briefcase. "But who bopped Bjornsen?"

Maybe H. J. and the Timberlake heiress jumped the guy and used the gun to club him with. If so, where had they gotten to?

He made his way across the chilly room.

The hall was empty, too. "H. J.? Mardy?"

There was no one out on the porch of the Victorian mansion. The station wagon, the Fiero, and his own car were all still parked down in front of the ramshackle garage.

Glancing toward his feet, he noticed a slip of folded white paper lying next to the balding welcome mat. It was the map the realtor had given them.

Now, though, there was something written on the back of the memo page. He bent, making himself briefly dizzy, and grabbed it.

"Juster" was written in pencil in H. J.'s familiar scrawl.

"Juster? Where the hell did he come from?" Ben went back inside the house. "More important, where did he go?"

$\triangledown$

24

BEN GAMBLED. ON WHOM to call and on what voice to use.

Sitting in the parlor of the old mansion, with the unconscious Bjornsen spread out before him, he made his first phone call.

Juster's sister answered on the third ring. "Hello?"

"Hi, sweetheart," he replied in his Don T. Timberlake voice.

"Mr. Timberlake, I wish you wouldn't use expressions like that."

"Bingo," he said to himself. To Linda Albright he said, "Sure, sure, love. Now let me talk to Mark."

"Mark's not here, Mr. Timberlake. He left to get ready for his meeting with you."

"And that's right where I'm having a problem, dear," he explained in the lazy nasal voice. "I wrote down everything about the location on a slip of paper, and now I can't seem to find the damn thing. Fill me in, can you?"

"Well, yes. He's going to be at the McNelly Gardens."

"Right, I remember now."

"In the caretaker's house just inside the gates."

"It's all coming back to me, hon."

"A friend of Mark's is the regular caretaker, but he had to

go to Florida unexpectedly for a few days and so Mark's housesitting. That's why he picked the place for your meeting. You know, the gardens have been closed to the public for nearly five years. A real shame, too, because—"

"Hey, sweetheart, if we don't quit schmoozing I'll be late for the damn meeting."

"But that's not for an hour yet. You have—"

"Got to go. Bye." He hung up, leaned back for a few seconds. "Good guess. Couple of them, in fact. Juster has been in contact with Don T., and Juster's sister knows a lot more about things than she let on this afternoon."

He picked up the phone again and punched out another number.

"Willmur Emergency Services," answered an efficient-sounding woman.

"This is Dr. Mackinson," Ben said in his E. G. Marshall voice. He gave her the address of the mansion. "There's a patient here in the parlor with a serious head injury, and we'll need an ambulance at once."

"Can't you get him to your own hospital, doctor?"

"That's, unfortunately, quite impossible." He repeated the address. "Please, don't delay."

After hanging up, he turned on several lights, then took his leave.

"This isn't like you, Mark," said Mardy, sounding disappointed.

"Yes, it is. You really don't know me all that well."

"What this amounts to," pointed out H. J., "is kidnapping."

"Nonsense," said the lean, bearded photographer, who looked nothing like Lincoln. "I've merely escorted you to a business meeting."

"The fact that you've escorted us against our will, toting a gun," H. J. told him, "is really going to impress a judge. He might not think too much of your slugging Bjornsen either."

The three of them were in the cozy living room of the caretaker's house at the edge of the McNelly Gardens.

H. J. and Mardy shared a fat, flowered sofa. Juster, holding a snub-nosed .32 revolver, was in a black leather armchair.

"Once Mardy talks to certain people," he said, "she'll realize I haven't really done anything illegal."

"Possibly, but *I'm* sure as heck going to stick to my original opinion."

The blond asked, "What is this all about, Mark?"

"Somebody wants to meet you."

"Who? What are you talking about?"

H. J. said, "He's not running an escort service. I imagine one of the Timberlakes is coming here to look you over."

"That name was mentioned back at the Shatsworth house," Mardy recalled. "Who are they?"

"Soap," said H. J.

"They're a very wealthy family," said Juster.

"And why would they want to meet me?"

H. J. started to reach for the briefcase, which Juster had brought along. It was lying on an end table. "If you skim through this stuff, you'll—"

"Leave that where it is," ordered Juster.

Shrugging, H. J. sat back. "Your pornographer friend found out that you're probably an heiress."

"A what?" She looked from H. J. to Juster.

"Maybe," he said. "Just maybe."

"C'mon, you know you believe she is," said H. J. "How did you find out?"

"I'm not completely certain even now, so—"

"Lloyd Dobkin must've let something slip. He did talk to you, didn't he?"

"As a matter of fact, yes. But that was really just to arrange for the use of some of my shots in *Bare*."

"In *Bare?*" asked Mardy. "You actually sent pictures of me in to a sex magazine?"

"What the devil did you think I was going to do with them?"

"Use them in a book of artistic shots, that's what you claimed."

"No, I never told you anything like that."

"My God, thousands of men staring at—"

"Naked is naked, Mardy. Whether you call it art or porn. You knew damn well that people would be looking at those—"

"You contacted the Timberlakes, didn't you?" H. J. eyed him.

Juster glanced away. "Well, yes."

"And someone is coming here to meet you."

"Very shortly."

"Then here's something to think about," she said. "Back in Brimstone, Connecticut, my hometown at present, a fellow named Larry Dahlman was murdered—he was Lloyd Dobkin's brother-in-law. I had the notion that whoever stole the folder that's in the briefcase also murdered him."

"What's this got to—"

"Just now, though, we had a long chat with the fellow who admits taking the folder. He swears he didn't kill Larry at all."

Juster frowned. "The man is probably lying."

"He may be," admitted H. J. "If he isn't, though, then somebody else did Larry in. And that somebody could well be one of the Timberlakes."

"Bravo, sweetheart. That's a neat piece of reasoning." A small, dark man had stepped into the room.

He walked up to the seated Juster, pressed the barrel of his .45 automatic to the back of his neck, and took the revolver away from him.

$\triangledown$

25

Ben APPROACHED THE CARETAKER'S house from the rear, after having climbed over the high, rusty wrought-iron fence that circled the fifteen acres of public gardens. The day was fading away, and a frail mist was starting to drift along the weedy pathways.

Looming up huge on his right was an immense turn-of-the-century greenhouse, all glass and iron. Many of its dusty panes were cracked. Atop it, several shadowy birds were just settling down to roost.

Doves, Ben surmised. Or possibly pigeons.

On his left ran a series of high hedges that had once represented a parade of topiary animals. Unclipped for years, the participants had long since lost their original shapes. In the misty dusk Ben could discern a great hulking creature that had once been an elephant. Ahead of it slithered a shaggy blur that might have been an alligator long ago.

There were lights on in several of the rooms in the two-story wooden house. An outside staircase went from the backyard to the dark second-floor porch. Ben made a note of that in passing.

Then, as he neared the front of the house, he all at once

tripped over something. He fell, sprawling across it on the grassy pathway.

What he'd fallen over was the body of a lean, bearded man. There was enough light spilling out of the nearby house for him to see the bullet wound in the dead man's temple.

He gingerly untangled himself from the body and crawled a few feet away into the shadows of the shaggy animals. "Jesus, this must be Mark Juster," he realized. "And H. J. was with him."

Off in the shadows, just beyond the last overgrown beast, a foot scraped on gravel. "Who's that over there?" a rough voice demanded.

"I've never," Don T. Timberlake informed them, "had much patience."

"Where's Mark?" asked Mardy.

"Outside, sweetheart."

"There was a shot."

Timberlake, who was sitting in a wicker rocker with his automatic resting in the palm of his right hand, smiled at her. "That's right," he confirmed. "But right now, hon, I've got to have a look at your ass."

"Suppose," said H. J. from the flowered sofa, "she's not Sue Ellen Timberlake?"

"Won't make a hell of a lot of difference," he told her. "I'm going to have to get rid of the lady anyway. You, too, love. But I'd like to satisfy myself as to whether she is or not."

"You and your sister aren't behaving in a very cordial way."

"That bimbo? Hell, Laura doesn't know a damn thing about this."

"And how did *you* find out?"

"I picked up a few hints from friends in the media that Lloyd Dobkin was digging into something pertaining to the missing kid," he replied. "I contacted Larry Dahlman, a longtime buddy, and asked him to find out more about what exactly was going on."

"Did you tell him to kill Dobkin?"

"No, dear, that was entirely his own idea," said Timberlake. "Not a bad one actually, except that Larry then decided he could take over all the material his brother-in-law had collected and sell it to me. Enterprising, but way too greedy of him."

"So you killed him?"

"Had it done."

"You never got hold of Dobkin's file, so you must have found your way here some other way," H. J. said. "Juster contacted you, didn't he?"

"Exactly, sweetheart. His problem was he thought he could hold me up the way Larry had tried to do," said Timberlake. "His asking price was lower, but it struck me that getting rid of the bastard was a much simpler course." Smiling thinly, he rose up out of his creaking rocker.

"So you double-crossed him."

"Sure, dear." He pointed at Mardy. "Let's take a look at that birthmark."

She shook her head. "No, I won't do that."

"I've got a fellow named Miguel Garcia resting his buns out in the Porsche, sweet," he explained. "I can have Miguelito come in and hold you down while I lift your skirt. Thing is, he's liable to hurt you quite a lot while that's going on."

The young woman looked at H. J.

H. J. told her, "You might as well."

"All right."

"Smart move." Smiling, Timberlake thrust the .45 into his waistband and rubbed his hands together.

Moving deeper into the concealing shadows of the high hedge, Ben called out, "Who the hell do you think it is, asshole?" He used Don T. Timberlake's voice.

"Mr. Timberlake? I thought you was in the house with the women."

"Obviously I'm not," he said. "Now explain to me why you left this stiff here."

A tall, lean man appeared around the edge of a shaggy topiary beast. He was slightly hunched, squinting into the shadows that concealed Ben. Resting in the crook of his arm was a shotgun. "Hey, you told me to leave him where he fell, and then we'd bring the van around after we took care of the women. Put them all in at once."

Ben said, "Well, asshole, I want him moved right now. Do you understand that?"

The man walked up to the body and crouched. "You know, Mr. Timberlake, I'm damn certain you told me not to—"

"Okay, drop the shotgun next to the body." Ben had moved up behind and was poking a just-found chunk of branch into his back.

"You aren't—"

"Quiet. Shed the damn shotgun."

"Okay, okay." He let it fall.

Appropriating the weapon, Ben discarded his branch. "Stay right there, don't make any noise," he advised. "Are there any other guards out here?"

"No, only me."

Ben poked him with the gun barrel. "You sure?"

"Yeah, just me and Mr. Timberlake came here. You don't have to break my frigging spine."

"Who are you, by the way?"

"Miguel Garcia."

"Thought I recognized the voice. Another chauffeur," Ben said, remembering having encountered the man in Manhattan a few days ago. "Put your hands behind your back, Miguelito."

Using his own belt, Ben tied the man's hands behind him. He utilized Garcia's belt to truss up his ankles. With the chauffeur's handkerchief and his own necktie he fashioned a gag.

"Be back for you later," he promised. He headed for the

outside stairs that led up to the dark second floor of the house.

H. J. pointed out, "It could just be a coincidence."

"Makes no difference," said Timberlake as he returned to his rocker.

Mardy, dressed again, was sitting forlornly in an armchair, hugging herself. "You mean I . . . that I'm not who I think I am?"

Glancing at his watch, Timberlake said, "It's time to be moving along, girls."

"You must be curious," said H. J.

"About what?"

"About whether or not Mardy actually could be your missing cousin."

"She's got the damn butterfly birthmark on her ass, honey."

"Sure, but suppose there's no possibility she really could be Sue Ellen?" prodded H. J. "If, for example, she remembers her real parents or that all her records show—"

"Are you stalling, for some reason?" He left the chair, turning the automatic in her direction. "In hopes, perhaps, that that clown you used to be married to will come riding to the rescue?"

"The idea had crossed my mind, yes."

"Well, you can—"

"Matter of fact," said Mardy quietly, "I was adopted. Sort of."

Timberlake scowled at her. "What do you mean, sort of?"

"I was raised by my . . . Well, I thought she was my aunt. Her name was Hazel Cranford, and she passed away three years ago," explained the young woman. "A month or so before Aunt Hazel died, she told me that I hadn't been adopted by her in any official way. My birth certificate, my baby records were faked. So were the stories she'd told me about my parents dying in auto accident."

Timberlake inched closer to her. "So who the hell are you?"

"My aunt told me, or so she'd always believed, the daughter of her brother. That is, a daughter born to a woman he wasn't married to."

"What was this wayward brother's name? Cranford, too?"

Mardy shook her head. "No, Cranford was her married name. Her brother was Matt Reinmann."

"Wow, another chauffeur." H. J. sat up straighter.

Timberlake asked her, "What are you nattering about?"

"Apparently you aren't up on your family history," she told him. "Since I've just read Lloyd's account of the Timberlake kidnapping, I remembered the name. Matt Reinmann was your uncle's chauffeur. He wasn't suspected of anything at the time, and he died of a sudden heart attack about a week after the little girl was taken."

Mardy said, "Yes, he did die right after he left me with his sister."

Timberlake sat down again. The wicker rocker groaned. "He kidnapped the damn baby, stowed it with his sister, and then dropped dead before he could make a try for ransom. Christ almighty."

H. J. said, "She really is Sue Ellen Timberlake."

After a few seconds he announced, "It isn't going to do her a damn bit of good."

"Wouldn't it be wiser to accept her as one of the family?"

"Don't try to bullshit me, dear. People are already dead, so we can't gloss over this." He stood. "Besides, I've already decided that there are enough Timberlakes in the world. We don't need one more."

"Unfortunately, you're not the only one who knows about her," reminded H. J.

"I'll remedy that and—"

"Don, you little putz!" came a voice that sounded like that of Laura Timberlake Barks. "What in the name of god are you up to now?" She sounded as though she were coming downstairs from the second floor.

Surprised, Timberlake turned to stare toward the open doorway.

H. J. yanked up a table lamp and smacked his gun hand as he turned away from her.

Timberlake howled, dropped the automatic, cursed.

Before he could stoop to retrieve it, she booted him in the crotch from behind.

While he was doubled up clutching himself, she took possession of the gun.

Carrying the shotgun, Ben stepped across the threshold. "It worked," he said.

"Yep, even though your Laura wasn't all that great," said H. J.

"It was," he said, grinning, "sufficient."

$\triangledown$

26

THE EVENING OF JUNE 13 was warm and clear. The Sound out beyond the windows of Orlando's restaurant was calm.

"It's depressing," remarked H. J., sipping her white wine.

"Thirty-two is nothing," Rhonda Sankowitz assured her. "In fact, anything in the thirties is still great."

"I can also recommend the forties highly," added Joe Sankowitz.

Ben was watching the water. "When I was a kid, I figured I'd be rich and famous before I was forty," he said. "Turns out I was right."

"Fame is fleeting," reminded the cartoonist. "Last week, after you turned Don T. Timberlake and his minion over to the authorities, you were celebrities. 'Foil tycoon, find heiress!' trumpeted the tabloids. This week, though—"

"This week we're in *People*," reminded H. J. "And the local papers wrote us up because we also blew the whistle on Eva Dahlman Dobkin and her love-crazed driver."

"Okay, but by next week you'll be nonentities again. That's the way the world works."

Rhonda patted H. J.'s arm. "Is the Timberlake heiress actually going to give you folks a handsome reward?"

H. J. nodded. "Yeah, and she also told me she's going to

set up a fund for me to help finance my new career as a gallery painter. Specific amounts haven't been worked out yet."

Joe asked, "But she doesn't actually have any money yet, does she?"

"Laura has accepted her as the real thing and given her access to a bank account of her own while all the legal angles are being worked out," explained Ben. "She has money."

"And she really is the baby who was carried off way back then?"

"Yep, they've pretty much established that."

"All I have on my backside," complained the cartoonist, "is calluses."

"He does," confirmed his wife.

Sankowitz turned to H. J. "Now that you've solved another mystery and earned a handsome, we hope, reward, are you going to retire from getting into messes like this?"

She smiled sweetly and took another sip of wine. "From now on I intend to live a life of reclusive probity," she assured him. "I'll get started on that soon as we come back from Hollywood."

"Hollywood?"

Ben said, "Our fleeting notoriety reminded some people out there that I was a dependable voice man. They want me to do the lead voice for a new animated cartoon show."

"Which one?"

"It's based on a comic strip about a chicken, thing called *Dumb Cluck.*"

"Doesn't sound like a PBS series," said his friend.

"Pays better, though."

Sankowitz leaned back in his chair. "Los Angeles," he said slowly and thoughtfully. "And you're going along with him, Helen?"

"I am."

"You can get into all kinds of messes out there," he said.

"That's true," she agreed.